looked around again for Bridget and that's when I saw him. He walked in and went straight for the pool tournament sign-up sheet. He scribbled his signature right under my name. I planned to win that tournament, which had a two thousand dollar cash prize, so at first I was just sizing up the competition.

When I looked at him, my heartbeat reacted like the snap of the first break, ricocheting in controlled chaos.

Love in the Corner Pocket

MARLENE PEREZ

Point

YA
Perez

Copyright © 2008 by Marlene Perez

Library of Congress Cataloging-in-Publication Data
Perez, Marlene.
Love in the corner pocket / Marlene Perez.
p. cm.
Summary: Chloe, a Laguna Beach, California, high school student, sorts out questions about her parents' separation and her own friendships and love life as she gets ready to compete in a pool tournament.
ISBN-13: 978-0-545-01991-0 (alk. paper)
ISBN-10: 0-545-01991-5 (alk. paper)
[1. Interpersonal relations—Fiction.   2. Friendship—Fiction.
3. Divorce—Fiction.   4. Pool (Game)—Fiction.   5. Laguna Beach
(Calif.)—Fiction.]   I. Title.
PZ7.P4258Lo 2008
[Fic]—dc22   2007042090

12 11 10 9 8 7 6 5 4 3 2 1   8 9 10 11 12 13/0

Printed in the U.S.A.
First printing, May 2008

Book design by Alison Klapthor

ING
5.29
02-09

To Michelle, who is the best best friend anyone could ask for
and who played many games of pool with me

Acknowledgments

To Abby McAden, my amazingly funny and talented editor, who snatched victory from the hands of defeat. Thanks to Mary Pearson, Cathy Atkins, Lynette Townsend, and Debby Garfinkle for their great critiques. Thanks to my agent Stephen Barbara, whose positive attitude makes things happen. And finally, thanks to my husband and children, who put up with my weird ramblings and love of working in my pjs. And thanks especially to the divine Miss M., who reads every manuscript.

Chapter One

$\mathcal{I}$ was just a girl in a pair of low riders who might give them a glimpse of my thong when I bent over to take a shot. Or that's what guys thought when they first played pool with me. They asked me for a game so they could stare at my ass. Guys don't *seriously* think that a mere girl can beat them at pool.

A game of pool is full of deceit. Otherwise, no one would put their money on the table, would they? I mean, if a guy knows from the beginning that I'm going to run the table, why would he play?

Since my dad left, I've had a no-guy rule. It helped me focus on the game. I hadn't even indulged in a random hookup, at least, not until Alex.

The first time I saw him was at Gino's, on a hot Friday afternoon. It was late October, well after school started.

My friends and I went to Laguna Beach High School, in Orange County, California, the place television had made famous (or infamous, depending on how you looked at it). But don't believe everything you see. Life was much less chaotic than portrayed on television, at least before Alex came into my life.

Laguna Beach isn't like what's shown on television, at least the Laguna I knew. The Laguna I knew was a sleepy little beach town nine months of the year. Lots of writers and artists lived here, along with a handful of celebrities who have prime beach real estate that they rarely use. The other three months of the year was when the aliens (also known as tourists) invaded our quiet little town. In the summer months, traffic was bumper-to-bumper, and even I couldn't get a table at Gino's.

Gino's was a restaurant on Pacific Coast Highway. Out of the big bay window, if you craned your neck, you could see both the sunbathers and the surfers paddling out to catch the waves. The tablecloths were red-checkered and those cheesy red glass candleholders snuggled up with the salt and pepper shakers. Most of the candles had melted down to nothing, but Gino never replaced them. It smelled like basil, yeasty bread, and spilled beer.

It was a dive, but we hung out there a lot. Gino never minded if we came in straight from the beach, tracking sand and dripping water everywhere. Gino's also had the best food in town. The best pool tables, too.

I was supposed to meet my best friend Bridget and some of our friends, but I was early, so I played cutthroat with a couple of college boys who pretended they knew how to shoot pool. They barely knew how to hold their cue sticks. I wanted to go over and correct their stances, but I restrained myself. They'd only take it the wrong way.

The forty bucks I'd win would be the start-a-new-cue-fund. I hated asking my mom for money. I called the eight ball and sank it, putting the college boys out of their misery. They left a few minutes later, looking like two scolded puppies.

I looked around again for Bridget and that's when I saw him. He walked in and went straight for the pool tournament sign-up sheet. He scribbled his signature right under my name. I planned to win that tournament, which had a two thousand dollar cash prize, so at first I was just sizing up the competition.

When I looked at him, my heartbeat reacted like the snap of the first break, ricocheting in controlled chaos.

He saw me watching him and smiled. That's all it took. It was the same cocky grin that Tom Cruise had in *The Color of Money.* The rest of the package, his sparkling gray eyes, his curly black hair, his broad shoulders, that was all icing. My brain refused to listen to what my body was saying.

When he reached up and took a cue from the rack on the wall, I held my breath. Gino was going to go ballistic. The guy in the T-shirt must not have seen the sign, the one that promised pain and suffering to anyone who touched those cues.

Gino only let a few people keep their cues on that wall and nobody else was allowed to touch them. I didn't have a cue hanging on that rack and Gino's was my second home. Gino always said, "Be patient, your time will come."

I jumped when Gino, who was sitting at his stool at the bar, let out a great roar and came rumbling over. I thought he was going to pulverize the guy, but instead he wrapped him in a great big bear hug.

"Alex, when did you get back in town?" Gino said.

Alex, his name was Alex.

Gino steered him in the direction of the kitchen. "Wait until Rose sees you."

I watched their receding backs with a little sense of panic. What if this was the first and last time I saw him? My hormones were all dressed up with no place to go. A swift charge of lust went through me, like electricity zapping through a wire.

Maybe Gino felt my eyes boring into his back, because he stopped and turned around. He couldn't possibly miss me, since I was standing there with my mouth open. I'm pretty sure I looked as intelligent as a guppy.

"Chloe, I want you to meet my nephew," he hollered.

I wiped the palms of my hands on my jeans, hoping the material would absorb the sudden coating of sweat.

Gino practically dragged the guy over to meet me. I was worried that he would think I was a troll or something. I frantically tried to remember the last time I'd washed my hair. This morning. Fantastic. I was safe from greasy hair.

Alex snagged a mint from the big jar of peppermints on the counter. I grinned.

I remembered I'd been snarfing down a slice of spicy pizza and fished in my pocket for a tic tac. Gino made a mean white pizza, heavy on the garlic.

Potential bad breath or not, it seemed like this moment was meant to be. It was like the soft second before I sunk the eight ball or the rare times when I knew I had played a perfect game.

He was taller than me, not too much taller, though. Then he touched my hand and I swear a sizzle started in my blood. "I'm Alex Harris," he said.

"You look familiar," I said. *You look familiar? Could I have sounded any stupider?*

"Alex is an aspiring actor," Gino said. "Maybe you saw him in a commercial." He said it in the same tone he'd use to describe someone who'd skipped out on a bar tab or cheated at pool. Uncle Gino clearly wasn't a fan of his nephew's chosen profession.

Alex held my hand a second longer than strictly necessary. We were the only two people in the room. Then I noticed Gino grinning like a fiend and immediately dropped his hand. We stood there, smiling at each other.

"Chloe, there you are," a voice said.

Three minutes into our relationship and Alex already had to take the acid test. Bridget.

My best friend was a golden girl. She glowed from the sun, her blonde beauty dazzling everyone within view.

We first met at the beach when we were about three. We both wanted the same sand shovel. We were locked in combat when our moms came and pried us apart.

"That's *my* shovel," Bridget said. "Give it to me and I'll be your friend." She smiled the sweetest smile, and I remember thinking that she was the most beautiful girl I'd ever seen.

I let go of the shovel and she took possession of it with a happy sigh. I immediately burst into tears and hid behind my mom.

Bridget waddled over and handed me the shovel. She put her arm around me. "Don't cry!"

But I only cried harder.

"Here, you take it. I'm sorry," she said, her dimples dancing.

But I didn't want the toy anymore. I just wanted Bridget to be my friend.

So when she came over with that same look on her face, I knew that Alex was something she wanted.

My discomfort intensified as she eyed him like a chef eyes a particularly fine filet mignon. I could see the "fresh meat" lightbulb appear above her head.

Bridget was tall with a killer body. I was the opposite. Bridget called it petite. I called it bony. Bridget said my long dark hair was dramatic. I called it mousy.

She was more than a gorgeous blonde; she had that indefinable *something.* She was so far out of my league, I was barely on the same planet.

Alex said a polite hello and then resumed eye contact with me. He didn't seem to notice that the quintessential California girl was standing in front of him.

Bridget smiled at him, but his eyes were focused on mine. It gave me goose bumps.

"So, Chloe," she said, not taking her eyes from Alex, "Theo's saving you a place at the table."

I stared at the floor. I remembered that the old Chloe, the one who believed in true love, was gone. It was time to make a swift exit and leave the playing field to Bridget.

"I gotta go," I muttered. "Nice to meet you." And then I practically ran. I didn't hear whatever Alex called after me.

But I heard her giggle and his low rumble of laughter in reply.

Chapter Two

The rest of the group was at our usual table. I pulled up a chair next to Theo, so my back was to Bridget and Alex. Kayley and Vinnie were glued together, as usual.

"What happened to Bridget?" Theo said. He got grumpy if he didn't eat regularly, like eight times a day. He burned the calories off. I'd played about a million games of beach volleyball with him and the guy had a serious six-pack.

I jerked my head in the direction of Alex and Bridget.

"Hey, weren't you talking to that guy a few minutes ago?" Kayley said. She looked a little like a redheaded porcupine. "I don't see why you're friends with her when she acts like that."

"Bridget can't help it. Boys are just automatically dazzled by her." What I didn't say is that Bridget was there for me when my dad left. When I heard the news, I couldn't breathe. I remember gasping for air and then, later, Bridget's voice comforting me.

"Not *every* guy," Kayley said, gesturing to the two at the table.

"Vinnie's completely in love with you," I said. Vinnie nodded in agreement. "And Theo's immune," I continued. "Dating Bridget or me would be like dating his sister or something."

Theo looked up and frowned. He'd been text-messaging someone, probably a girl. Theo was one of the cutest guys in our high school, and it was a mystery why he didn't have a steady girlfriend.

"Hey, I know that guy," he said, looking over at Alex.

"He's Gino's nephew. His name is Alex. How do you know him?" I said, trying to sound casual.

"Summer after sixth grade," Theo said, looking at me like that was supposed to be meaningful.

"You mean the summer Bridget and I went to camp?" I got the chicken pox and she got the cutest guy in camp. I spent all my time in quarantine, itching and scratching the entire time, and sending long whiny letters home to my older sister, Nina. Bridget spent all of her time with the hotter than hot Scott Stevens, but when no one was looking, managed to sneak me funny care packages full of red Twizzlers, Zingers, and details about their hot romance.

"That's right, you weren't here when Alex showed up last time," Theo said. There was an edge to his voice.

"What happened?" I said.

"Nothing," Theo said, but he watched Bridget and Alex with narrowed eyes.

I changed the subject. The waiter interrupted my reverie and we ordered a cheese pizza. We never waited for Bridget. She always ordered a salad anyway. She was on some weird diet because she was an actress and worried about how the camera added ten pounds.

And there was no way I was going back there to ask her and watch her charm Alex.

"Don't change the subject," Kayley said. "Go back there and talk to him. You saw him first."

"Kayley, quit bossing her around," Theo said. "Maybe she wasn't interested."

"Oh, she was interested all right," Kayley said, snuggling back against Vinnie.

Bridget sauntered back to the table, looking like a self-satisfied tabby.

"Dibs on that," she said, tilting her head toward where Alex still stood.

She moved fast. It seemed like only a minute ago, I was introducing them. Oh, wait, it WAS a minute ago.

"Bridget, that's not fair," Kayley said. "Chloe was talking to him until you horned in."

Bridget smiled down at me. "Sorry, Chloe," she said. "I didn't notice."

"That's because you weren't paying attention."

Kayley gave her an angry stare. The rest of the group looked at me, slightly pityingly, I thought.

"Why don't we arm wrestle for him?" Bridget offered me her arm, her eyes twinkling at me.

"If I wanted him, I could have him," I said, suddenly tired of the unspoken assumption that all she had to do was smile and I was out of the running.

"You could?" Bridget said. When I glared at her, she said hastily, "I mean, of course, you *could*. It's just that you don't."

My heart sank. Bridget was interested in Alex and she was a fast worker. I kind of *grew* on guys or something. Worse, she didn't think I was any competition at all.

The rest of the table looked surprised at her bluntness, but she grinned.

The waiter showed up with a deliciously cheesy pizza and before I could say anything else, Bridget surprised me by eating a slice.

"I can't resist," she said, putting a slice on her plate. Some of the cheese dripped off the side and Bridget swooped it into her mouth. "Do you know how long it's been since I've had any cheese? God, I *love* cheese. I wish I could find a guy that I loved as much as I love cheese."

"How long does it take to find someone to love?" I said.

"Two weeks," Bridget said. "That's how long it takes me to find someone."

"He may have a different idea," Theo pointed out calmly. "You can't force him to like you."

"I don't have to," she returned cockily.

Kayley raised a skeptical eyebrow, but didn't say anything. She wasn't Bridget's biggest fan, but it was a fact she usually managed to conceal.

"Most of your relationships haven't lasted two weeks," Kayley said.

"We all can't find true love at seventeen, like you and Vinnie," Bridget said caustically. "How long have you been going out again?"

Kayley ignored the question, with good reason. They'd been going out for two months tops.

"What's true love anyway?" I said.

"Three little words," Theo said, looking me in the eyes. "I love you."

"What?" I said. My pulse jumped.

"He has to say 'I love you,'" Theo explained. "That's how you know."

"What if he says it to more than one person?" Kayley said. "Some guys hand out 'I love yous' like most people hand out chocolate."

"Not all guys," Vinnie said softly.

Kayley snuggled against him like a satisfied cat. "Yeah, not all guys."

"But remember Jacob Marsh? He waffled between my sister and Heidi Wassermein their sophomore year. I would never want to go through that." I shuddered, remembering the havoc created by that little love triangle. It took Nina a long time to get over Jacob. She was in college now, far far away from all the high school drama.

"Well, I wouldn't tell a girl I loved her unless I meant it," Theo said.

I said, "It's hard to meet a guy. The right guy, anyway."

Theo crossed his arms. "It's not if you're looking in the right place." He sounded pissed for some reason.

What was his problem? I gave him a hurt look, but he avoided my eyes.

"You make it sound so easy," I said, feeling defensive.

"It seems easy enough for Bridget," Vinnie observed.

"So what? Bridget's better at flirting than Chloe," Kayley said. I winced. "Sorry, Chloe, but it's true," she added.

Kayley was right. Bridget could wrap a guy around her little finger, make him twist himself into a pretzel for the privilege of bringing her a glass of water.

"Look," Bridget said, "it doesn't matter." She threw an arm around me. "Boys are easier to find than seashells. Chloe and I will be best buds no matter what happens."

I threw my arm around her and grinned. "She drives me crazy sometimes, but I love her." She had convinced me that everything would be okay.

It was true. Friendship with Bridget wasn't all sunny skies, but I wouldn't trade her for anybody else. It was hard to be best friends with such a gorgeous girl. I hoped that a little of her glamour would rub off, but no luck so far.

I thought that Alex would probably fall under her spell within the week and I would go back to my quiet little life.

"Kayley, want to grab a game later in the week?" I said. I needed the practice and she took playing pool almost as seriously as I did.

"Sure," she said. "Give me a call and we'll set something up."

After dinner, we said good-bye to Vinnie and Kayley, who were gazing soulfully into each other's eyes and clearly wanted a little alone time. Outside the restaurant, Theo blushed and stammered, looked at his watch, and finally blurted out that he had somewhere else to be.

We watched him leave and I said, "Theo was acting weird, don't you think?"

"I think he had a date," Bridget replied. "Lia's after him."

Lia was a friend of Bridget's, but I didn't under-stand what Bridget saw in her.

"A date with Lia? Really?" It wasn't that Theo wasn't cute, because he was, but Lia Cruz didn't seem like his type. And I'd become used to Theo's company.

"Are you okay?" she said. "Are you mad at me about something?"

I smiled at her. "No, everything's cool."

"Okay," Bridget replied, linking arms with me. "Just because your parents screwed up, doesn't mean you'll follow in their footsteps," she said, snapping her gum. She was up for a gum commercial and had started chewing gum nonstop.

"Oh, and I have such a great track record." Actually, I didn't have a record at all.

"Rich Edmunds has a thing for you," she said, "but you won't give him the time of day."

"I know," I said. "No one at school interests me." I hoped she'd pick up on my subtle hint that I was inter-ested in somebody now, but apparently not.

"I think you're making a mistake, but it's your life. Besides, that means more for me." Bridget flipped her hair back from her face.

I looked at my watch. "I'd better get home. I still have homework."

My mom was a pain in the ass about grades. I had to maintain a B average or no car in my future. I've had my license for ages.

I thought I'd get my car when all the separation guilt kicked in for my dad, but so far, no deal. He always backed my mom in every argument and she thought that I wasn't ready for the responsibility of my own vehicle. Of course, she still thought I needed someone to cut my food for me.

"I'd give you a ride," Bridget said, "but I had to park about a million miles away."

"I don't mind. It'll help me burn off the pizza."

"Like you need to worry," Bridget said, and then, because Bridget was Bridget, she added, "I still think you're making a mistake. You can't shut romance out of your life forever."

The Santa Ana winds were blowing and my hair was everywhere. I pushed it out of my eyes. Long hair was a pain, but secretly, I thought it was my one good feature. I dug into my pocket, found a rubber band, and used it to put my hair into a ponytail.

We passed by the old-fashioned soda shop where I'd spent the summer scooping ice cream into giant waffle cones. My mom made me quit before school started again. Business died down in Laguna when the tourist season ended anyway, but I would have liked to finish out the summer.

Bridget spent her summer volunteering at the Pageant of the Masters. She modeled every year. This summer, she posed for the Vermeer painting *Young*

Woman with a Water Pitcher. I still couldn't believe that she managed to stay completely still for so long, but she looked incredible in her costume.

There was an art gallery every three feet in downtown Laguna, crammed in between surf shops, restaurants, and clothing boutiques.

We passed by the gallery where my dad exhibited his paintings. Dad was a major player in the art world. He's the one who taught me to draw, but my sketchpad had been gathering dust lately.

I used to love his stuff, when it was all moody night scenes and storm-drenched beaches. It sounded mean, since he's my own father, but now there's something cookie-cutter and soulless about his work.

Things started to change even before Dad moved out. Now it seemed like people only bought his work because it went well with their new décor.

"Is that your dad's?" Bridget asked, pointing to an oil painting, another pretty sunset.

"Unfortunately, yes. It's more of his sofa art." I stopped in front of the painting.

"What do you mean?" she said.

"Paintings people buy to match their couches. Not that there's anything wrong with sofa art," I added quickly, remembering that her dad and stepmom had recently bought one of Dad's paintings, "but he is capable of so much better."

On the other hand, the only thing I had painted lately was the spare bedroom.

"I like your dad's new stuff," Bridget said airily. "You don't have to think about it. It's pretty and it sells well. What's not to like?"

I stared at her for a minute. Sometimes, I didn't get my best friend.

Chapter Three

$\mathcal{I}$ dragged myself out of bed on Monday. As much as I dreaded it, I needed to talk to Bridget about the Alex situation.

I didn't want to chance him coming between the two of us, but I thought he might be someone I could really like. I wanted to know if she liked him, too. I was confident that I'd talk to Bridget and everything would work out.

I wasn't like Bridget. I couldn't charm the entire student body with a smile. I needed to keep the friends I had.

Our lockers were right next to each other, so I tracked her down before class started. She leaned against her locker, flirting with Reid Medina, a senior and captain of the basketball team.

I loitered, as inconspicuously as possible. I didn't want to interrupt Bridget in action. Finally, when I had given up and opened my locker to pull out my English lit book, Bridget turned to me. She had a huge smile on her face.

"Guess who asked me out?"

I glanced over to where Reid stood, surrounded by a cluster of letter jackets. He had the dazed look of one of her conquests. When he saw us looking his way, he grinned and gave a little wave.

She licked her lips. "Tasty, isn't he?"

"So you like him, then?" I said, trying to sound casual.

"I do like him," she said.

I smiled at Reid approvingly. He was the answer to my problem. If Bridget liked Reid, then the Alex thing was a nonissue.

"Besides," she continued, "I've never dated a basketball player. He has such big — hands."

"Bridget!" I said, pretending to be shocked, before we collapsed into a heap of giggles.

The tension in my spine eased. I hurried to class, confident that my problem was solved.

Morning classes went by quickly. I had a test in English lit and when the bell rang for lunch, we all gathered up our stuff, ready to bolt before Ms. Lucas could assign any homework.

I saw Bridget in the hallway and waved, but she didn't see me. She walked by without a glance, her hand entwined in Reid's. He pulled her close and whispered something in her ear, which caused Bridget to blush. She never blushed.

I shrugged. Bridget's absorption in Reid was good news for me, even though I was hurt that she'd forgotten me so completely. I hoped she'd forgotten about Alex as well, which would leave the field clear for me.

I had an hour for lunch, enough time to walk to Gino's for a quick practice game. Gino's wasn't crowded, so I got a table right away. Afterward, I went to the counter to order.

"Two slices of veggie, please," I said without looking up.

"Hi, Chloe," Alex said.

My head snapped up. "What are you doing here?"

"Helping my uncle," he said. "He owns the place, remember?" he added teasingly. Alex handed me my order and I inhaled the smell of oregano and roasted eggplant.

"How could I forget? He has the best pizza in town. But aren't you supposed to be in school?"

He gestured to an empty table. "Not exactly. Got a minute?" he said.

"Sure." He sat across from me and watched me eat my pizza. In between bites, I asked him, "So why aren't you in school? Did you already graduate?"

"I'm a senior," Alex said, "but there was a mix-up with my transcripts. It should be all straightened out by next week. I'll be going to Laguna Beach High. That's where you go, right?"

Things were definitely looking up. "That's right, I do."

"Maybe you can show me around when I get there?" he said.

"I'd love to," I said, studying my shoes because I didn't want him to see the elation flooding through me. "And speaking of school, it's time I get back." I stood.

"Did you drive?" he said.

I shook my head. "No car. My mom is ridiculously strict about it."

"Then let me give you a ride back. I'll just let my uncle know I'm leaving."

He went into the kitchen and came back out a minute later jingling car keys. He was parked in the alley behind Gino's. He opened the passenger door of a shiny black Mercedes and then slid behind the steering wheel.

"Nice car," I commented.

He made a face. "Parental bribe," he said tersely, but didn't elaborate.

As we pulled into the parking lot, I caught a glimpse of Bridget and Reid. She was walking away from him at a fast pace. He had his hands stretched out pleadingly. It looked like they were fighting already.

I crossed my fingers and prayed that Bridget's notoriously short attention span would hold a little while longer, at least long enough for me to entrench myself with Alex.

"Thanks for the ride," I said. "See you later."

He said, "You can count on it."

The words sustained me for the rest of the week. I spent the days hoping I'd run into him again. I didn't see him at Gino's or school, and Friday came without another sign of him.

That night, when I went into the living room, I passed by the empty spots where my dad's favorite paintings used to hang.

My mom was sitting by the phone, figuratively speaking. She was pretending she was ever so busy, plumping pillows and dusting, but I knew waiting by the phone when I saw it. She wore ratty old sweats that hung on her. When Dad lived with us, Mom would wear grubbies to write in, but she'd always change into something nice for dinner.

"So the great Devon McBride didn't bother to call?" I said.

"Chloe, don't call your father that. You know I don't like it," my mother said.

"It is his name," I said, in what I thought was a reasonable tone.

She sighed. "I know you're angry at him. But he's still your father."

"He sure doesn't act like it." I turned away. We'd been over this before. Me ragging about my father and my mother defending him. Lather. Rinse. Repeat.

When the phone rang, I ran to answer it before she could.

"Hello, McBride residence. Chloe speaking."

"It's me."

"Hey, Bridget," I said. We lived up a hill off Laguna Canyon Road, which meant sporadic cell phone reception. I wouldn't trade it for anything, though.

Mom said jokingly, "It's a record. You two haven't talked in ten whole minutes." She pretended to clutch her heart, looking at her watch. She was clowning around, but I could tell she was disappointed that it wasn't the great Devon McBride.

"Funny, Mom," I said, then turned back to the phone. I tried to ignore my mother hovering in the background.

I tried to pay attention as Bridget raged about Reid, but my mind was on my parents. Things hadn't been good between my parents for about a year before he left. They were overly polite to each other at breakfast, using pleases and thank-yous like they were weapons.

My dad started spending nights and weekends "painting" and Mom stopped smiling and muttered that maybe it was time that he slowed down and acted his age.

A few months later, my dad rented studio space in L.A. "because of the commute." His studio was more like an assembly line. My dad would paint a couple of brushstrokes on a piece and then his "students" would finish the piece. I thought it was completely phony. My dad touched something with his almighty paintbrush and suddenly it was an original?

Right. Who did he think he was kidding? Apparently, a lot of people, since collectible "McBrides" were all the rage.

"Chloe, are you even listening?" Bridget's voice brought me back to the present.

"Sorry, Bridget, I didn't catch the last part," I said.

"Sorry if I was boring you," she said sharply. Then her voice softened. "You'll find someone, too."

"It's not that," I said. "My dad is back in town."

There was silence on the other end of the phone. "That's not such a big deal, is it?" she said. "I mean, after all, he is your father."

"No, it's not a big deal," I said, stung.

"Don't be like that, Chloe," she replied, then, "I've got to go, there's someone on the other line. Talk to you later."

I stared at the phone for a minute.

"I couldn't help but overhear your conversation with Bridget," Mom said. She put her finger to her lips and chewed the end of the nail.

"Mom, quit that. They'll never grow if you bite them," I said.

"I've been meaning to tell you, but from what I heard, you already know that your father is here for a few weeks."

I didn't say anything, and my mom continued nervously, "I know he wants to see you, but he's been very busy since he arrived."

"Yeah, I bet he has," I said.

"He does want to see you," she protested softly. "He just doesn't want to upset you."

"A little late for that, don't you think?" I wanted to take the words back the minute they were out of my mouth. It wasn't my mom's fault, none of it was.

"Do you want something to eat? There's pasta," Mom changed the subject.

"You've been writing again?" I motioned to the smudge of ink, but then I realized that it wasn't ink on her cheek; it was some sort of sauce.

She touched her cheek. "It's not ink," she said. "It's just dinner."

My mom was the worst cook. She used to embrace the fact that she was the creative rather than the domestic type, but since Dad left, she'd been making all these really weird, trendy dishes involving disgusting food like caviar and portobello mushrooms. No more frozen pizza or Cheetos. She didn't even buy Cheetos anymore.

I wish Mom would confine her creativity to her writing. I'd been eating entirely too much of her maple fried salmon. I could use a good solid meal. Thank God for Gino's or I'd starve to death.

Lucky for me, I could eat anything and get away with it. Bridget said that I could model, but I know she was only saying that to be nice. My legs are long enough to be a trip hazard, but not as long as hers. But then again, I just don't measure up to the Bridget yardstick. I'm not sure why I even try.

Chapter Four

I was beginning to think that my dad was a figment of my mother's imagination. On Saturday, I still hadn't heard a word — not a call, not a visit.

"Chloe, I'm going grocery shopping. Do you want anything?"

"Cheetos," I said, but I wasn't holding my breath.

"What kind?" Mom said. She was in a good mood. Cheetos had been banished when Dad moved out.

After Mom left, I grabbed my backpack and headed for Gino's. Maybe I'd see Alex there and coax him into a game or two.

It was almost Halloween and Gino had gone all out. Jack-o'-lanterns grinned from the window, and ghosts and bats floated down from the ceiling.

Alex wasn't behind the counter, but I snagged a table in the back and grabbed the rack. I practiced a particularly tricky jump shot until I thought I had the hang of it.

"Your mom told me I might find you here." I recognized the voice immediately. The great Devon McBride finally made an appearance. He had acquired a permatan, like that sunbaked old guy on the commercials. His skin was the color and texture of a Sunkist orange.

He held out his arms, but I ignored them, choosing to lean against the pool cue instead.

"You look taller," he said finally.

"That's what happens when you leave," I said. "People change." Even with the tan, he looked the same. He looked like the guy who had spent hours teaching me the right way to hold my pencil. He didn't look like the kind of guy who left, but he was.

"I'm back now," he said.

"That's what Mom said." I knew I sounded like a brat, but I couldn't help it.

"I missed you, honey," he said. "I'd love to see what you've been working on."

"You're looking at it," I said. I bent down and took a shot, avoiding his eyes.

"You're not drawing?" he said.

I shook my head. "Not for a long time."

His voice rose. "That's a waste of your talent and you know it."

"What do you care?" I bent down and took another shot, but my hands were unsteady and I missed. God, I was such a bitch. No wonder he left.

And as if to prove me right, when I looked up again, my dad was gone.

*   *   *

The weekend ended without any further word from my dad. At school, I felt a little lost. Whatever Bridget and Reid had been squabbling about, their tiff was over. They couldn't be pried apart with a crowbar. I'd had lunch with her once since Reid had appeared on the scene, and that was only because he was home sick that day.

Everyone in school was talking about the hot new guy. Guess who? Bridget told me that Alex was in her drama class and I tried not to worry. But I did.

I looked at the clock. I was in American government. They were in drama class right now, probably rehearsing some romantic scene from *Romeo and Juliet* or something.

Kayley leaned over and said, "Vinnie, Theo, and I are going to Taco Bob's for lunch. Want to come?"

"I usually eat lunch with Bridget," I said, "but she's been eating with Reid every day."

"You can bring her, too," Kayley said, "if you must." But she softened the statement with a smile. "Meet us in the parking lot at Theo's Jeep."

When the bell rang, I hurried off to look for Bridget, but, as expected, she was already with Reid. If she'd been flirting with Alex in drama, she wouldn't be hanging all over Reid, would she?

I practically skipped down the steps to the parking lot.

Vinnie and Kayley were in the backseat.

"Where's Bridget?" Kayley asked, but she sounded relieved.

"She had other plans," I said. "Let's go. I'm starving!"

Taco Bob's was a favorite lunch spot for our high school. The food was better than the fast-food places and you could get a steak burrito for three bucks. Needless to say, it was always crowded, but the owners were tolerant of the bunch of high school kids who descended upon them like a swarm of locusts, eating everything in sight and leaving as quickly as they arrived.

"Let's grab a table outside while the guys get the food," Kayley said.

"Good idea," Theo said. "Chloe, what would you like?"

I handed him a ten. "Two steak burritos, a soda, and an order of fries."

He waved away my money and he and Vinnie went to stand in line.

Kayley spotted a table outside. "C'mon, before someone else takes it." She hurried over and sat down.

She looked at me curiously. "So why haven't you and Theo ever hooked up?"

"What?"

"You heard me," she said.

"We're friends," I said. "Just friends."

"Simmer down. Your face is getting all red." Kayley looked amused.

"What's so funny?" I demanded.

"You are," she said. "You sounded so indignant just now. It's a fair question. He's unattached, you're unattached. He's gorgeous and obviously into you."

"He is not," I said. "He likes me, as a *friend*. Besides, I'm not Theo's type."

"What's his type?" Kayley asked.

For a moment, I was stumped. I hadn't seen Theo with anyone lately. "Well, he likes smart girls. You know the type, tortoiseshell glasses, spouts poetry, and plans to go to Stanford or Yale."

"You're smart," Kayley said.

I shook my head. "Not like that."

"Besides, what's wrong with going out with a friend?" Kayley said. "Seems like you would already know his bad points."

"Theo doesn't have any bad points," I said.

"So why don't you go out with him?"

Alex's face popped into my head.

"No chemistry, I guess," I said. It wasn't true. I had wondered what it would be like to go out with Theo, but I couldn't risk it. He was a good friend and I couldn't risk losing him.

The guys came back a minute later, weighed down with our lunch. Theo put the tray down and handed me a burrito and a churro.

"Dessert, too," he said.

"Thanks," I said. I leaned in to inhale the smell of fried dough, cinnamon, and sugar. "I love churros."

Kayley nudged me meaningfully, but I ignored her.

Theo said, "Did you hear about the tournament?"

"What now?" Kayley said.

"Not enough players signed up for a nine-ball tournament. Gino decided it's going to be eight ball only."

"Straight pool? We'll get a bunch of bangers," Kayley said.

"Hey, I started out as a banger," Theo said indignantly. "I'd hit the ball as hard as I could and hoped that something went into a pocket."

We all laughed at that one.

We ate heaps, but there was still food left on the table when we were finished. "I'm so full," I said.

"Do you want your churro?" Vinnie said. He eyed it longingly.

I wrapped it back up. "I'll save it for later."

"She's a bottomless pit," Theo said. "I don't know how you stay in shape."

"Clean living," I replied.

Theo snickered. "Are you doing anything Friday night?" he said. "Because my mom is out of town and I'm having a Halloween party."

"Oh," I said. "I'm not big on parties."

"Bridget is invited, too," Theo added quickly.

"It'll be fun," Kayley said.

"I'll try to make it," I said, but they all gave me skeptical looks. "I mean it this time."

Kayley snorted, but then smiled at me. "We don't mind that you're a tad antisocial, Chloe. Theo *does* have an awesome pool table, though."

"Don't let it get out that I have to lure girls to my house with my pool table," Theo said. "I couldn't stand the humiliation."

Who was he planning to lure to his house?

Taco Bob's was starting to empty out. I looked at my watch. "Thanks for lunch, but I have a quiz in French class, so I need to get back."

By Friday, I still hadn't decided whether to go to Theo's party when Bridget called me.

"Did you hear about Theo's Halloween party tonight?"

"He invited me at lunch the other day," I said.

"Do you think you can bust out of jail?" Bridget was so funny, ha ha. Everyone was a comedian.

"Well," I said, "I still have homework and I was going to watch a movie." I thought about my DVD of *The Hustler*, an oldie starring Paul Newman. It's my favorite movie. There aren't that many movies out there about shooting pool. It's not your typical teenage movie material, but then again, I prided myself on being anything but typical.

But I needed to get out of the house. Lately I'd been spending my weekends the same way, hanging out with my mom and pretending that we both weren't waiting for Dad to come back.

I glanced over at my mom, who acted like she wasn't listening to my conversation. I took the phone and went into the other room. I knew Mom wanted to follow, but she made a valiant effort and restrained herself.

"I'm not really in a party mood," I said in a low voice. "Why don't you come over and we'll drive by the *Nightmare* house? We haven't gone yet this year and it's almost Halloween."

Bridget and I both love Halloween. Every year, one of the houses a couple of streets down had a *Nightmare Before Christmas* display with these huge cutouts of Jack Skellington and Sally. It was our favorite display and we never missed it, even after we were too old for trick-or-treating.

One of the things I loved about Bridget was that she never made fun of me or tried to convince me to drop my childish pleasures. I loved the *Nightmare* display and Bridget knew it.

Maybe Bridget would come over and hang out. Not likely, though. It was Friday night and she had a very active social life.

As expected, she had other plans. "You know I love you, but Reid is supposed to be there. Come to the party. We'll go to the display tomorrow night, I promise."

I wondered if Bridget expected me to hang out by myself all night while she and Reid stared into each other's eyes.

But then an idea occurred to me. If Bridget was meeting Reid, she'd be occupied if Alex showed up.

"Okay, I'll go, but I don't have a costume."

"Bring that white dress of Nina's. I have an idea for costumes for both of us."

"I can only stay for an hour or so."

"You have to stay longer than an hour if you want to impress anyone. You're not chickening out already, are you?"

"No, I'm not chickening out," I said glumly. "It's my curfew." Mom had given me this ridiculous curfew and, since the separation, she enforced it to the second.

"Ask if you can spend the night. We'll go to the party. Technically, it won't be a lie. We'll end up at my house eventually."

"I don't know," I said.

"She practically chains you to your bed." Bridget sounded more melodramatic than usual, but she was up for a part in a new television show. She'd be playing the crazy daughter of that star who'd been nominated for an Emmy all those times but never won.

"I'll call you back," I said and hung up the phone. I usually avoided the sheer stupidity of the high school party scene in Laguna, but a night at Theo's sounded better than spending the night hanging out with my mom, which was a truly pathetic line I'd already crossed more times than I wanted to count.

I called downstairs. "Mom, can I sleep over at Bridget's?"

She didn't answer me, but I could hear her talking. I followed the sound of her voice. She was on her cell phone and had that note in her voice that told me it was my father. He finally called or maybe Mom had finally caved and called him.

"I'd love to. I'll see you there." My mom's voice was low. She was practically whispering into the phone. Hmm. Interesting. If I didn't know any better, I'd say she had a date. I hoped it wasn't with my father.

She jumped about a foot when she saw me standing in the doorway.

"Do you need something, honey?" she said. I noticed that a bandanna covered her hair and a smudge of ink dotted her cheek. She looked like she used to look, back when she was writing all the time, and for a minute, I thought my old mom was back.

I repeated my question. "Can I stay over at Bridget's? Her parents are out of town."

To my surprise, my mom said yes. She nodded absentmindedly. This was not my mother. It was too easy. Something was going on.

"I'll give you a ride," she said. "I'm going out anyway." She tried to act like it was no big deal, except her smile told me she hoped that Devon McBride was here to stay.

Chapter Five

The party was starting to sound appealing. Anything to get out of the house, and maybe Alex would be there.

Everything I owned looked boring, and my sister Nina, who usually helped me find a hip outfit for social occasions, was at college. I was counting the hours until the stylish one in the family would return home and offer me some advice.

"Are you ready?" The sound of my mother's voice snapped me out of my reverie. I was still in my sweats, but Mom would get suspicious if I got all dressed up for a night at Bridget's.

"Almost! I'll meet you in the car," I called down. I crept to Nina's room and stuffed her white dress and gold ballet slippers into my overnight bag. I ran downstairs. I didn't want to give Mom time to change her mind.

When my mom pulled up to the gate guarding the Stewart house, I hopped out and punched the security code for the electronic gate.

"Bye, Mom!" I said as I shut the car door. I tried waving her off, but she wouldn't budge. When the gate swung open, she motioned me back and I hopped back in to be driven to the front door. My mom was so overprotective. It was ridiculous.

"I think I should speak to Bridget's dad first," she said. "Or her stepmother."

"Mom, I told you that they were out of town," I said. I knew she was testing me.

She frowned, but didn't stop me from opening the door. "When will you be home tomorrow?"

"I don't know."

"Chloe —" she started, but I put my hand up to stop the lecture.

"Around four tomorrow afternoon," I said.

"Nice try," she said. "Lunchtime, no later. Your grandma is coming over."

Mom always got tense around Grandma and it didn't help that since Grandpa died, my grandma had become harder and harder to deal with.

I bit back an exasperated sigh. I wanted to remind her that I was *sixteen*, not six. I was almost seventeen, as a matter of fact, but lunchtime was vague enough. It'd give me a little leeway. I knew that if I complained, she'd make it even earlier.

I jumped out and walked to the door, hoping against hope that my mom wouldn't expect to come in with me. It would be too embarrassing. Fortunately, she stayed there, watching me until I made it through Bridget's front door.

"What took you so long?" Bridget demanded.

"Give me a break. You know how my mom is."

Bridget gave me a hug. "We should start getting ready."

I looked at my watch. "The party won't really get started for at least another hour."

"Yes, but I do want to look good." Bridget opened her closet door and peered in.

I rolled my eyes. For Bridget, looking good meant two hours of preparation. "Fine, but didn't you say you already had ideas for our costumes?"

She spent the next half hour obsessing over what to wear. "I've been dieting all month and I still didn't get the part," she said, throwing another outfit on the floor.

"Sorry, Bridget," I said. "Your big break is coming, I'm sure of it." Bridget was a fantastic actor. I didn't envy her talent, but I envied that she knew what she wanted and she went for it. I wanted to be a little more like her.

"I'm bummed," she said. "It was a part in a movie. Orlando got a part, though. He e-mailed me. We could have spent all that time *rehearsing.*" She wiggled her eyebrows suggestively.

I cracked up. Bridget didn't even *know* Orlando, so it was highly unlikely he'd e-mailed her, but she made me laugh.

No guy, not even Orlando, could keep the notoriously fickle Bridget's interest for too long. Reid better stay on his toes. Two weeks was an eon in Bridget time.

I knew that the sooner we left, the sooner Bridget would find her boy-of-the-week-club selection and I'd be off the social hook. I hoped for Reid's sake, he was still in the club.

If Alex didn't show and the party sucked, I could sneak back to Bridget's, put my sweats back on, and go to bed.

I had already changed into my costume, which was the white dress I'd borrowed from Nina's closet.

"So what was your idea for our costumes?" I asked her.

"Goddesses," she said. "We're going as goddesses. That white dress will be perfect, and you can borrow anything from my closet to dress it up."

I rummaged through Bridget's closet, looking for something to jazz up the plain white dress.

"Can I borrow this?" I asked, holding up a slim gold belt.

Bridget nodded and I wound the belt around my waist, ran a brush through my hair and slipped on Nina's gold ballet slippers. If anyone asked, I was Fortuna, the Roman goddess of chance.

Bridget disappeared into her enormous walk-in closet. I flopped on the bed. I felt itchy. I hated waiting. I wanted a cue stick in my hand, but Bridget's family didn't own a pool table, just a pool.

I flipped through the pages of a magazine, turned on her television, turned off her television, picked the polish off my nails, applied new polish to my nails.

"Bridget, are you ready yet?" My nails were dry and there was still no sign of her.

"Almost," she hollered back. That was Bridget speak for another half hour.

I turned on the radio, thumbed through her music collection, played a CD, but there was still no Bridget.

"Bridget, hurry up! You don't want to keep Mr. Wonderful waiting too long or someone else will snag him," I said.

She finally emerged from her closet. She had on skyscraper heels and a clinging blue costume with a deep vee in the bodice and a long slit up the skirt. She was Venus, goddess of love, and she looked breathtaking.

"Do you like it?" she twirled around. "It was the last one the costume shop had."

Suddenly, I hated my makeshift costume.

"Don't be mad," she said. "I got it as a backup, and I knew you wouldn't go if I made you shop for costumes, too."

I softened toward her. "The guys don't stand a chance," I said.

"I officially hate you," Bridget said. "It took you all of ten minutes to get ready and you look good, even though that dress makes you look like you don't own an ass."

I winced a little. She was right, I didn't have much of a butt, but it hurt when she pointed it out. Bridget's butt, of course, was perfect. Bridget's lack of tact was one reason that not many girls liked her. The other part was that she was absolutely gorgeous, and who needed that kind of competition?

"Thanks, Bridget, but you look great, too." She always looked beautiful. If she weren't my best friend, I'd hate her.

"What are you talking about? I'm not even close to being ready."

I should have known.

I felt completely underdressed. I tugged on my dress. My flats felt too babyish, my hair too simple, and my costume, which I had thought was cool, now seemed boring and sloppy.

I told myself that I wasn't competing with my best friend. It's a good thing, too, a snarky little voice in my head reminded me, because she kicks your ass in the looks department.

Bridget sat at her vanity and applied eyeliner.

"Here, let me do your eyes," she said. "And I found some gorgeous earrings to go with the whole goddess look."

She went back into her closet and I sighed. I couldn't stay mad at her, even though I felt like somehow she'd manipulated me. On the other hand, I'd probably never socialize without Bridget there to nudge me along.

She came back with two tinsel tiaras and put one on my head. "There, the finishing touch." Then, "Let's go. Reid will be waiting."

She put a hand up to her hair and fluffed it. "My hair just won't behave. Tonight of all nights." She snatched up a bottle and squirted a tiny bit of liquid into her hands, then smoothed it over her hair before looking into the mirror again. "That's better."

I stopped in my tracks. "You're nervous," I accused. "You're never nervous. You must really like him."

"I really do," she said. "I do like him, more than anyone I've ever met. I just hope he likes me." She smiled softly and headed for the door.

"How could he not?" I said. "He's lucky to have you."

She gave me a wink. "Maybe it'll be a lucky night for both of us. Maybe you'll meet someone, too."

"Maybe I already have," I said, but Bridget had already left.

I followed her as she cut across her neighbor's lawn. I walked slowly. I was dreading the party, but I knew Bridget would be mad if I flaked out now.

My slippers sunk into the lawn and left deep imprints. My shoes would end up covered in mud and somehow, miraculously, Bridget's little sex-kitten heels wouldn't show a speck of dirt. I didn't know how she did it.

She was my best friend, but sometimes I wished I'd win at some competition with her. The only thing I was good at was pool, and Bridget wouldn't play with me anymore. But when we were both in sixth grade, it was all we talked about.

I said, "A party doesn't seem like Theo's style."

"What do you have against Theo anyway?" she said. "It's not like . . ." her voice trailed off.

I finished the sentence for her. "It's not like anybody else is interested? Is that what you were going to say?"

"No, that's not it at all. Forget I said anything," she replied. "Let's not fight. We're here to have a good time."

I nodded, but inside I was fuming. Why was she assuming I didn't have any other prospects? What about Alex?

I knew Theo liked me, but I wasn't sure why. It wasn't like I was even nice to him half the time. Dating him would be as comfortable as wearing my favorite sneakers.

I hunched my shoulders against the wind. It was cold and I hadn't brought a coat. Theo's house was the kind of house everyone called "architecture." It was all sharp edges and angles, and hung suspended on the side of the cliff as if daring gravity to do its worst.

It was practically all windows and every light was on. There was already a crowd dancing in the living room.

When we walked in, I started choking on the thick curtain of smoke that hung in the air. Herb, not nicotine. I made a face. I couldn't stand the smell of weed. And then there was the added trauma of coming face-to-face with a costumed Cheshire cat smoking a bong.

"Where is Theo's mom again? It's going to take at least a week to fumigate the place when this is over," I yelled over the booming stereo.

"What?" Bridget shouted back.

I shrugged, giving up on the idea of actually conversing for the rest of the night. We pushed our way through the wall of bodies, into the family room. The lights were low and couples were intertwined on the sofas.

We backed out and returned to the crowded living room. I made a drinking gesture to Bridget and pointed to the kitchen, where I assumed the keg was located. Bridget stayed behind, scanning the crowd. I knew she was looking for Reid, so I left her there and headed for the refreshments.

I walked over and opened the kitchen door. And that's when it hit me.

I gasped as a torrent of sticky orange liquid drenched the front of my dress. Worse, it was ice cold.

I stared up at Theo. I realized I'd collided with him as we both went through the kitchen door. Some of the liquid had dripped onto the floor and I slipped. Theo grabbed me as I fell. He slipped an arm around me to steady me, and I was surprised at how muscular his arm was.

Wipeout punch was my guess. A favorite at LBHS parties, the traditional recipe for wipeout punch was vodka, Kool-Aid (orange this time in honor of Halloween), lemon-lime soda, and whatever other ingredients you could sneak out of the house without your parents catching on.

I reeked of alcohol, and when I looked down I saw there was a huge orange stain on Nina's white dress. I was dead. Nina would kill me. Her dress, the one I'd borrowed without permission, was ruined. It was the dress she'd worn when she had been crowned Queen of the Frost Ball.

My white cotton bra was outlined underneath the dress. I might as well have not been wearing anything at all. I crossed my arms over my chest and tried to wipe the Kool-Aid off. I grabbed a handful of my hair and started wringing the sticky stuff from it.

I glared up at Theo.

"I'm so sorry," he said. "I didn't see you. Let me help you." He started dabbing me with a dish towel.

I smacked his hands. "Hands off!" I snapped.

Theo realized where his dish towel had been and blushed as red as cherry Kool-Aid.

Then Alex walked into the kitchen. Just who I wanted to see when I looked like a disaster.

Chapter Six

He grinned at me and said, "Chloe, I was wondering if I would see you here."

He looked amazing in a black leather jacket and jeans. Underneath the jacket, he wore a faded black cotton T-shirt with "Vince" in white letters. His hair was slicked into a three-inch-high pompadour.

A laugh escaped me. We shared the joke, knowing that nobody else got it.

Vince, the cocky young pool hustler, was Tom Cruise's character in *The Color of Money*. That's when I realized I wanted Alex no matter what. Pretty stupid reason, huh? Because of a shirt? But that's what happened.

Bridget was going to be so sorry she missed this.

He stopped in the doorway. I was surprised to see Lia Cruz as she ran right into him. Lia was dressed as a Playboy bunny.

"Are you okay?" Alex said.

"What happened to her?" Lia said. "She looks like something the cat dragged in."

Original, huh? And talk about cats, Lia was practically meowing. Why did the girls at my school have to be so catty? I couldn't compete with her if I tried.

Alex was the cutest guy in the whole damned town. Lia had just met him, but was already plastered up against him like a second pair of underwear.

I glanced at Theo, who was dressed like he usually did, except for his bright orange T-shirt that read, "All work and no play makes Jack a dull boy." Over and over again. It took me a minute, but then I realized it was a quote from *The Shining*.

I wondered how he felt about Lia cozying up to Alex, especially since she'd just gone out with Theo last weekend.

The rumor was that Lia had gotten breast implants over summer break. I tried not to stare at her chest, which was displayed in her low-cut costume. She had the best body that daddy's money and a judicious use of purging can get you.

"What are you looking at?" Lia said.

I blushed and stammered, "They, I mean, you, look nice tonight."

She did, too, even though it was completely obvious that she was wearing a costume designed to highlight her new purchases. Lia's implants looked almost natural. The rumor also said that her dad had forked over a small fortune for the best plastic surgeon in L.A.

She smiled at Alex, but then put a hand on Theo's arm. "I'm cold," she said.

When Theo smiled at her his eyes lit up, and I wanted to rip that fuzzy tail right off her. I repressed the thought. I had absolutely no right to be jealous of Lia.

Alex said, "What happened to you?"

"A run-in with some lethal party punch," I said.

I ran my hand through my hair, which dripped sticky stuff all over the carpet.

"I'll get you a blow-dryer," Theo said. "You can clean up in my room."

Lia frowned, generating annoyance. "But, Theo . . ." she said.

"It's okay, Lia," he said. "Hang on a minute. Let me get Chloe situated and then I'll give you a ride." He turned to me. "Lia's car won't start so I'm giving her a ride home."

"Oh, right," I said. Like that wasn't the lamest excuse I'd ever heard.

Lia gave me an evil look behind Theo's back.

"I can give Lia a ride," Alex said.

She brightened and immediately glommed on to Alex's arm.

Theo and I walked back through the living room, up the stairs, and down the hall to his room.

His room, as usual, was spotless.

He switched on a light and headed for the bathroom.

He came back with a couple of towels and handed me one. I went to sit on the bed, but then remembered the state of my clothes and straightened up.

A dark maroon comforter covered the bed. I noticed the gray flannel sheets I'd helped him shop for last month.

He'd taken down all his posters, but his books still lined a tall bookcase.

"Your room is nice," I said. I smoothed the comforter nervously. Alone in a bedroom with a guy. Nerve-wracking.

"With your help," Theo said, cocking an eyebrow at me.

"Yes," I said, "but I like the way it all came together."

He grinned. "Good. It was about time I did something with it. The teddy bears were killing my image."

I couldn't help myself. I stared at the king-sized bed and wondered exactly who he had brought up here. The image of Theo, shirtless, kissing some girl, flashed into my mind before I could squelch it.

I couldn't look him in the eye after that visual, so my gaze wandered to his desk, complete with a laptop and charging station. Nice guy or not, I'd bet anything that the names and cell phones of half the girls in town were in that computer already. My fingers itched to find out. Even Lia had been chasing Theo, at least until Alex showed up.

"Your dress is soaked." Theo said. He started to towel off my soaked outfit, stopped himself, and handed me the towel.

"Maybe you should wear some of my sweats until your clothes dry. I'll throw your clothes in the dryer." He glanced down at my stained outfit. "Uh, I'll throw it in the wash first."

He went over to the dresser and rummaged through it. He handed me a T-shirt and some sweatpants.

"I'm going to change," I said. "I'll be right back."

I went into the bathroom and stripped off my sister's ruined dress. My bra was completely soaked. I shrugged and stripped it off, too. I threw it in the sink and ran the cold water and rinsed the Kool-Aid off the bra. When the water ran clear, I blotted the worst of the stain.

I toweled dry and held Theo's shirt up to my face and breathed in. I could detect no trace of Theo, only the smell of freshly washed cotton. I threw on the shirt and tried to figure out what to do about my bra.

I couldn't casually hand my bra to Theo for laundering. Somehow, I'd sneak it into the dryer later. Maybe Lia would still be around to distract him. It wasn't like I had as much as she did up there, but I needed a sweatshirt or something to hide my lack of support.

A knock at the door made me jump. "Are you okay in there?"

"Yeah, sure. I'll be right out, but do you see a sweatshirt I can borrow? I'm kind of cold." No way was I explaining the wet bra to him.

"Sure," Theo said. A minute later, he tapped on the door. I opened it and he dropped a hoodie on the floor. It was red and white, with "Laguna Beach Artists" and the high school mascot stamped on the back.

I put on the sweatshirt. I stuffed my pitifully small bra into the front pocket. One problem solved.

I stared into the mirror. My face looked ghoulish in the fluorescent light, my hair was drying in clumps, and I had the beginning of a zit on my chin. I mentally compared my appearance to Lia's. She was a nine all the time and I was about a seven on my best day.

I shrugged. Theo was my friend, just my friend. I didn't need to impress him.

At least I came out of the bathroom decent.

Theo reached out to touch my face. I held my breath, but he only tucked a stray strand of hair behind my ear.

"I'll take your dress and put it in the washer," he said.

He laughed at my look of alarm. "Don't look so scared. I know how to do laundry," he said. "Okay?"

I nodded and handed him the sodden dress. Good looks and he could do laundry, too. I was impressed.

We went back to the party, but I didn't see Bridget anywhere. Lia was waiting by the front door.

"I'll be right back," Theo said to me. "Don't go anywhere." He walked away, in the direction of what I assumed was the laundry room. He stopped to say something to Lia. She looked mad. I kind of enjoyed that.

I turned away. There was something about the way they had been standing so close together that made my stomach churn.

I scanned the room for Alex. He wasn't there. I was betting someone else had already snatched him up and I wouldn't see him the rest of the night.

I stood with my hands in my pockets and watched the dancing. The noise made me want to tear off my ears. It looked like all of Laguna Beach was crammed into Theo's undoubtedly spacious house.

My chest felt like there was something pressing on it. How had I let Bridget talk me into coming to this too-loud, too-crowded excuse to hook up?

Part of me wanted to go back to Bridget's house, but for some reason, I lingered. I liked to pretend it wasn't because of Alex.

I wandered through the house, searching for an unoccupied corner. I finally found a quiet room. A couple of people were passed out on the floor, but other than that, the room was empty.

There was probably enough time to throw my bra into the dryer before I went looking for Alex, while pretending that's not what I was doing. Yeah, right. I had plenty of time. Like Alex was going to dump who-ever had latched on to him and make a beeline back to hang out with me. I decided to skip it. I'd go without for the rest of the night. It wasn't like I really needed a bra, and even I knew too much heat could ruin a bra.

I assumed Bridget had found Reid and would be otherwise occupied. I was slightly comforted by the knowledge that she'd lost interest in Alex.

I flopped down on a cushy leather couch. It was get-ting late. The room had a large sliding glass door, which looked into the backyard pool. Much of the party had moved poolside.

I stood up and watched the party through the win-dow. I saw Vinnie and Kayley, dressed as the King and Queen of Hearts. They spotted me and waved me over, but I didn't want to be a third wheel, so I shook my head and stayed inside.

I didn't feel like joining them, but I didn't feel like going to sleep either. I wondered if my mom was home.

I sighed and clicked on the television. Maybe mind-less TV would make me forget my parents' problems. It would take more than luck to get my parents back together. It would take a force of nature.

The show ended. I hadn't even paid attention to what I'd been watching. I looked at my watch again. It was almost midnight and there was no way I was going to see Alex again tonight. It was time for me to leave.

"Hey, do you mind if I watch with you?" My heart jumped when Alex sat next to me.

"Not at all." My grip on the remote tightened. My heart beat faster. Maybe Alex was interested in me, just a little bit.

"Your outfit is in the wash," he said, "and I think the stain is going to come out."

"Thanks." I was impressed. Another good-looking guy who knew how to do laundry. "I thought Theo was going to do it. You had to give Lia a ride home, remember?"

He grinned. "Theo did it instead. Her perfume was giving me a headache."

I choked back a laugh. I was sure that Lia wouldn't appreciate hearing that her very expensive, very exclusive perfume stunk.

I was channel surfing when I heard a familiar name. I couldn't believe it.

My jaw hung open as I watched the camera pan onto my father's face.

"What the hell?" I said. I leaned forward.

"Are you all right? You've been staring at the television screen for the last three minutes."

"I'm fine. Fine. It's — I had no idea he was going to do a commercial." My stomach rumbled, rejecting the pizza I'd gobbled for dinner.

There he was, my father, sitting close to the interviewer. He was promoting his new products. It was one of those late-night infomercials.

I knew he had signed some licensing agreement and his art was going to be on coffee mugs, coasters, and greeting cards. It was classic Devon McBride.

Alex squinted at the screen. "Who?"

I pointed to the screen. "My father, that's who. My father's on television and he didn't even tell me."

Alex stared at the tiny figures. "That's your dad? Wow," he said.

I shrunk low on the couch.

"Your dad is Devon McBride?" Alex said. "The artist? I heard he was starting his own clothing line."

"Yeah. Wow." I wanted to sink through the floor. His face was small on the wide screen and he was smiling as if he didn't have a care in the world. I wanted him to be miserable. He had too many styling products in his hair. It looked plastic.

I frowned. "I can't believe he's on television."

"Are your parents still — together?" Alex's voice interrupted my thoughts.

"No, they're separated. I haven't seen much of my dad lately." I leaned closer to the television. "Are those highlights?" I screeched.

"It's okay," Alex said. "I know how you feel. My dad embarrasses me all the time. Your dad has his own company. How cool is that? "

I gave Alex a small smile. "He used to be an artist, but now he doesn't even finish his own paintings."

"He's successful. You've got to admire that kind of drive. I know what it's like. I want to be an actor, but I take modeling jobs to make the connections, you know?"

He was trying to make me feel better, but it wasn't his dad on national TV shaking his moneymaker.

"Do you want to get out of here?" Alex said, after a quick glance at my face. "You look a little pale."

I nodded. He took my hand and pulled me up from the couch. I noticed he didn't let go of my hand. I didn't mind.

"Let's take a walk," he suggested.

I clicked off the television. A little male distraction was what I needed. Maybe this was my lucky break. I had a lot more practice playing pool than I did getting a guy to like me, especially a guy who looked like Alex.

Chapter Seven

We slipped out the slider door, cut through the backyard, and headed down to the beach. It was deserted, except for a couple huddled together near a bonfire. The air tasted salty and crisp when I breathed it in.

We walked along the beach, still hand in hand. We didn't talk. I breathed in the tangy night air and wondered what I should say to him, but he didn't seem to feel the need to talk.

We sat on the cold sand and looked up at the stars. The sound of the waves crashing on the shore soothed me.

When I shivered, Alex put an arm around me and pulled me close. I leaned into him. I knew I'd have to go home eventually, but I pushed my parents and their problems out of my mind.

I watched his face when I didn't think he was looking. He was incredibly good-looking, but he was sensitive, too. It was weird how comfortable I felt around him. It was like we'd known each other a long time.

He smelled of some other girl's perfume. I assumed it was Lia's, but I forgot about it when he kissed me. He tasted bitter, like stale beer, but my body went hot when he wrapped his arms around me. For a second, I wondered what my best friend was going to say about Alex and me, but then all thoughts of Bridget went out of my mind. I was no longer thinking, I was all feeling. Eventually, we were rolling around in the cold, wet sand, kissing like we didn't need to breathe.

The touch of his hands under my shirt brought back my common sense. That wasn't how I wanted to get Alex to like me. And besides, what did I know about this guy?

"This is a bad idea," I said, finally remembering to push him away. We both sat up.

"Why?" Alex said. "I think it's a great idea." He sounded sulky.

I kissed him again, briefly. "Because I've got sand down my neck and a few other places. Contrary to romantic myth, a deserted beach is not the best place to . . ."

"To what?" he said, grinning.

"To — whatever," I said.

I stared up at the sky for a minute, trying to control the urge to roll around in the sand with him again. To my body, it seemed stupid, but I still put out a hand to stop him when he leaned to kiss me again.

"It's getting late. I should go." I wanted to talk to Bridget. I'd be honest with her and tell her that I really liked Alex.

"If you have to." He pulled me to my feet. We headed toward Theo's, but then stopped under a streetlight a few feet away from the house.

"Can I walk you home?" he said.

I hesitated. "I'm staying at a friend's house. Her parents are out of town." That was a stupid thing to say. I didn't want him to think I was inviting him over for a sleepover. "Let's go back to the party," I added quickly.

"In a minute," he whispered, before drawing me into his arms and kissing me again. We broke apart long enough to exchange phone numbers and then headed back to the house. His hand was warm in mine, but I shivered.

As we neared the house, Alex casually dropped my hand. I looked up, startled. He put his hand in his pocket and I relaxed. Nothing to worry about.

"I'll call you," he promised. I smiled, but I noticed he didn't take my hand again.

I couldn't help the huge smile I wore as we walked into Theo's house. The smile evaporated when Bridget rushed up.

"Chloe," she said, "I wondered where you'd disappeared to." Her teeth were tightly clenched beneath her smile, and a chill went through me.

"Didn't Reid show up?" I asked, assuming that's why she was so pissed.

"He's here. Passed out under the dining room table, like the idiot he is," she snapped.

Alex looked from Bridget to me. I wondered if he could tell there was something wrong. I got the feeling he did, because he said a hasty good-night and took off. Bridget and I watched him leave, but neither of us said anything.

The party had died down. There were a few random couples making out on couches. The house was in need of some tidying, but wasn't totally trashed.

We went to find Theo to help with the cleanup. He was in the kitchen with Vinnie and Kayley, who were loading cups and bottles into trash bags. Theo was mopping up the floor, but I didn't look too closely to see what was under the mop. His face told me he was rethinking the party-while-the-parents-are-gone idea.

Finally, the house was in decent shape and we headed for Bridget's. On the way back, Reid seemed to be a distant memory. All she talked about was how cute she thought Alex was. I wish I'd been privy to that bit of information BEFORE he had his tongue in my mouth.

Bridget was acting weird. Her voice was brittle and she didn't seem to notice that I wasn't saying anything. She threw words at me instead of talking to me and when we got to her house, she practically slammed the door.

I couldn't help resenting the fact that Bridget was after the only guy who had showed the slightest interest in me in the last six months. Every guy in school wanted to date Bridget, so she could have her pick of guys. Why had she chosen Alex? She knew I liked him.

I touched my lips with my fingertips, remembering his kisses. Maybe Kayley was right and it was time I stopped worrying about my parents' lives and started thinking about my own.

It was dawning on me that I had the chance to get the guy for a change. The idea lingered in my mind as we got ready for bed. I put on my sweats and brushed my teeth.

"Bridget, are you okay?" I said as I climbed into bed.

"I'm tired." She turned her back to me.

"Did you have fun at the party?" I tried again.

"Did you?" She whipped the question at me.

Fun? Fun wasn't exactly the word I'd use. "I had an interesting time," I said. "Alex and I talked. I mean, he's just a guy." Even as I said it, I knew it wasn't true. I wanted to stop the lies that came tripping off my tongue, but I couldn't.

I had never lied to Bridget before and now I'd lied to her over a guy, something we swore we'd never do.

Why had Alex kissed me? And why hadn't I told Bridget about it?

"You talked, huh?" Her voice dripped with innuendo.

"I don't understand why you're so upset about this."

"I'm not upset," she said and clicked off the light.

Oh, my God. I was totally screwed.

Chapter Eight

The next morning, I got up early and left. Bridget was still sleeping, so I left her a note and used Grandma's visit as an excuse for my cowardice. I told myself I was being a considerate friend. Some considerate friend I was.

Grandma was already there when I got home. I shut the front door and yelled, "I'm back," but nobody responded. I heard raised voices coming from the kitchen. They were at it already. My mom and Grandma were like oil and water. I don't know how they had managed to survive in the same household until Mom reached adulthood. Or until she cashed in her college fund and snuck off to Europe. I don't think Grandma ever forgave her.

I eavesdropped from the hallway. I needed to know what kind of fight I was walking into. It sounded like the you-should-have-been-a-teacher-like-we-wanted fight, which wasn't as bad as you-ran-off-to-be-a-bohemian-artist-with-your-great-love-but-you-failed-at-that-and-your-marriage fight.

My grandmother, as usual, was doing most of the talking, if you can call scolding at the top of your voice talking. My mom, as usual, sat there, taking Grandma's criticism.

"I'm back," I said again, stepping into view. I had to distract Grandma before she really got going.

Mom jumped up from the kitchen table. "I'll make you some breakfast."

"I'll make it," my grandma said. "Your mother can't cook."

My mother's china cup clattered in its saucer, but she didn't say anything.

While my grandmother scrambled some eggs, Mom sipped her herbal tea and did deep breathing exercises, occasionally muttering a "stay calm."

It sounded like good advice, especially since Devon McBride was in town.

"Chloe, you look too thin," Grandma said. She gave me a hug. "What has your mother been feeding you?"

A loaded question. If I told the truth, I'd hurt my mom's feelings. If I lied, Grandma would catch me in it. She always did.

"I've been eating a lot," I finally said. "But no matter what I eat, I stay like this."

To my relief, my grandmother left early in the afternoon, after a parting shot at Mom.

Grandma stood and said, "I've got to go. I have a

date tonight." My grandpa has been dead for a long time, but Mom flinched when my grandma said "date." She left the room a minute later.

Grandma's gaze followed her out of the room. "Your mother reminds me so much of Earl," she said with a sigh.

Earl was my grandpa. I wrapped my arms around her.

"I miss him, too, Grandma," I said.

"Your mom has her head in the clouds like he did," she snapped. But she let me hug her for a long time before she got into her car.

I watched her big white Cadillac back out of the driveway. I don't know who was more relieved to see her leave, Mom or me. I loved my grandmother, but she could be exhausting.

Kayley called me a few minutes later and asked me if I wanted to go for coffee.

We settled on coffee at Diedrich's, a local chain that always smelled of freshly roasted coffee, cinnamon, and vanilla.

I ordered a large blended coffee and Kayley ordered green tea. We found a comfy couch and then Kayley spent ten minutes talking about how sweet Vinnie was, which was true, if a little repetitive. Listening to Kayley was still better than talking about my screwed-up love life.

But the pressure of keeping it a secret was too much for me and I told her what had happened with Alex at the party.

"It's about time you found a hot guy of your own," she said. "I'm glad you hooked up with Alex. You can't let your parents' problems ruin your life."

"It's not just about my parents, you know," I said. "There's Bridget, too."

"You didn't tell her?" she asked.

I shook my head.

"Chloe, you need to talk to her about it," Kayley said. "She's your best friend. She'll back off. Besides, I thought she was going out with Reid."

But neither of us really believed it. I knew it when Kayley asked me the next question.

"Don't take this the wrong way, but why are you and Bridget still best friends? You don't really seem to have that much in common," she said, then added hastily, "not that it's any of my business."

"Bridget has always been there for me. I'm not that good at making friends, not like you are. Or Bridget."

She snorted. "You need a little practice, that's all."

"It's not that," I explained. "Bridget is everything that I'm not."

"Or you're everything she's not," Kayley replied.

"It's not like that," I protested. "Bridget and I have been through a lot together. My parents splitting up . . ." My voice cracked.

I didn't mention the things I'd been through with Bridget, like the time she became bulimic to get a movie role that eventually went to one of Hollywood's lollypop-head teen queens. "She's always been there for me. We swore that we'd be friends no matter what."

"Then why don't you tell her about Alex?" she said. Because she's so easygoing, people dismiss Kayley as this airhead type, but she's amazingly perceptive.

I pushed away the thought of Alex. I wasn't going to talk anymore about him or how looking at him made it hard for me to breathe. "Let's face it. Bridget's probably got him drooling all over her by now."

Kayley started to say something, but I held up a hand.

"I know. Bridget can't help it. Guys gravitate toward her," I said. "It's not her fault."

Kayley looked like she wanted to say more, but instead changed the subject. "What about Theo? He's cute."

"Sorry," I said. "Theo's a nice guy, but I don't want to lose his friendship." I'd known Theo forever and he was too nice for the likes of me. He was the sun-kissed surfer-god type and my dad liked him, for God's sake. The romantic kiss of death.

"Don't take this thing with Alex too seriously," Kayley cautioned.

But it was too late. I already was.

I changed the subject. "Bridget and I are supposed to go see the *Nightmare Before Christmas* display tonight. Do you want to come? It's the last night. The entire street decorates their yards for Halloween, but the *Nightmare* display is our favorite."

Maybe Kayley and Bridget would get along better if they spent some quality girl time together.

"Sure," Kayley said. "I've never seen it."

"Afterward, we can hang out at my house and pass out candy to the trick-or-treaters," I said.

"What about Bridget?" Kayley said.

I deliberately misunderstood her. "Oh, she doesn't eat candy," I said, "but she'll be there, too."

At dusk, Kayley showed up on my doorstep, but there was still no Bridget. I tried her cell a bunch of times, but got her voice mail every time. She was still probably mad at me about the party.

"Maybe she's planning to meet us there?" I said to Kayley. "Let's walk. It's only a few blocks away."

When we got there, I saw a familiar blonde head and waved.

Then I saw she wasn't alone. She was with Alex and he was holding her hand. My stomach flipped itself inside out.

I made a little noise and Kayley looked over to where they stood.

"Don't worry about it," she said. "We'll go over and say hello and then we'll leave."

"No, it's okay," I said. "It's not over yet." But the six-foot-tall Jack Skellington smiled skeptically.

We walked up to where they stood next to Oogie Boogie.

"Hi, Bridget, Alex," I said, careful to keep my voice even. I noticed that he dropped her hand when he saw me.

"Chloe," Bridget said, "I was wondering if we'd see you here. Alex thought all this was a little childish, but I told him that it was your favorite part of Halloween."

"I tried your cell, but you didn't pick up," I said. "I thought we were going together."

"When Alex called, I left a message on your machine at home," she replied airily.

When Alex called? I tried not to let anyone, especially Alex, see that the information was painful.

"We were going to go down to the beach later," Alex said. "Do you want to come with us?"

I started to say yes, but Kayley spoke first. "No, thanks," she said. "Theo and Vinnie are coming over and we're going to hand out candy. Very juvenile, I'm sure *you* wouldn't be interested." I gave her a puzzled look that she ignored. That part was for Bridget, I was sure.

We stood there for a few minutes longer, but it felt awkward. I couldn't look at the two of them standing there, shoulders touching.

Finally, Kayley said, "We've got to go. Theo and Vinnie will be waiting."

"They will?" I said, as soon as we were out of earshot.

She held up her phone and punched in Vinnie's number. "They will as soon as I call them. It's okay, isn't it?"

"Sure, but why did you mention it in front of Bridget and Alex like that?" I didn't get it, until Kayley spelled it out for me.

"So Alex would know that he's not the only guy interested in you," she said.

"I already told him that Theo and I are just friends," I admitted.

"Unfortunate, but not unworkable." She sounded like she was planning some sort of military strategy. "That was bitchy of Bridget to bring him," she added.

I said, "Bridget didn't think about it when she invited him."

But I couldn't stop thinking about it. Why had Bridget chosen to bring Alex to the one place she knew I'd be? And why had Alex gone with her, especially after our kiss?

The question lingered in my mind the rest of the night. *It was only a kiss,* I told myself as I passed out chocolate to the trick-or-treaters.

When Theo and Vinnie came over, Theo was wearing a green sweater that brought out his hazel eyes.

"Look at you!" I said.

"What do you mean?" Theo said.

"You look gorgeous in that sweater." I stroked the fabric on his arm.

Theo gave me a goofy grin, but Kayley yanked on my arm and led me away.

"Now is not the time to flirt with Theo," she said. "I thought you were going to concentrate on Alex. If you flirt with Theo, you'll break his heart."

"I wasn't flirting," I protested. *Was I?* But Kayley was right. I needed to focus on Alex.

"I'd like to see Bridget lose this one," Kayley continued. "You let her have everything. You don't even try to compete."

"We have different interests," I said. "Besides, Bridget is my best friend."

"Well, she doesn't always *act* like it," Kayley said sourly.

I knew Kayley didn't like Bridget, but I tried to explain anyway.

"When I was eleven, my grandpa died. You hadn't moved here yet, but I was a mess. And Bridget was there for me." My voice shook a little.

Kayley studied my face for a second. "I'm willing to admit I might be wrong about her. I'll *try*," she said.

I smiled at her. "Thanks. You'll like her if you get to know her."

We ordered a pizza, from Gino's naturally, and I tried to figure out how to entertain my friends. I was used to Bridget being there to be the social chair of any occasion.

Kayley helped me fill the candy bowls with the treats Mom had left. Where was she anyway?

I tried not to think about Bridget and Alex. We went to the family room and hung out.

"How about a game of cards?" Vinnie said. He held up a deck. "Spite and Malice?"

"I'm not really in the mood for Spite," I said.

"Had your fill already?" Kayley said, but thankfully it was under her breath.

I whispered, "Bridget isn't trying to hurt me. She's trying to win." But I was saying it as much to myself as to Kayley.

Kayley and Vinnie answered the door when the trick-or-treaters rang the bell the next time, but I noticed they were gone a suspiciously long time.

"We're taking the next ones," I told Theo, "or we'll never get a game started."

The doorbell chimed a couple of times, but I didn't hear it open.

"Where *are* Vinnie and Kayley?" I said.

Theo looked at me levelly. "Where do you think?"

"Oh." Our eyes met and I looked away from the mischievous sparkle in his eyes. I beat a hasty retreat. In the entryway, there was no sign of the missing couple, so I opened the door and handed a huge handful of candy to a little Wonder Woman and a cowboy.

I snagged a couple of handfuls and took them back to share with Theo. When I got back, I saw that he had found an old Monopoly game and was setting it up, and that Kayley and Vinnie were back.

"So," Theo said casually, as he tossed the dice, "where's Bridget tonight?"

Kayley shot him a dirty look and Vinnie kicked his foot under the table.

I looked at them. "It's okay," I said. "Bridget's on a date with Alex. It's no big deal."

They all stared at me for a minute, then Theo said, "I landed on Park Place. Score!"

We continued the game and avoided the subject for the rest of the night, but it couldn't be avoided forever.

Chapter Nine

I slunk through the hallways at school all week, feeling like I had a big red L for Loser painted on my back. What made me think I could beat out Bridget for a guy?

My cell phone didn't ring and I was pretty sure I knew why Alex hadn't called me. Too busy with Bridget, no doubt. Round one to her, but the battle was far from over.

I still saw Bridget in the hall with Reid, but they were always fighting, so it wasn't a total surprise when she called me one night to tell me they'd broken up.

"It's me," she said, without preliminaries. "Can you talk?" She sounded stuffy like she had a cold. It dawned on me that she'd been crying.

"I can talk. Are you okay?" There was a series of sniffles on the other end of the line.

"I'm fine," she said, but she didn't sound fine. "Reid and I broke up." Bridget was crying. Bridget never cried, not over guys anyway. "He broke up with me, do you believe it?"

"Do you want me to come over?" I offered, feeling helpless. I didn't know how to help her.

She cried harder. "No, I just need some time alone right now. I just wanted to hear your voice."

"Call me if you want to talk," I said. But I knew she wouldn't. She hung up a minute later.

The next day, Bridget pretended like the phone call had never happened, like Reid had never happened.

"Have you seen Reid?" I asked her as we walked to class.

"Who?" She tossed her hair and smiled fetchingly at some poor freshman guy who didn't know what hit him. "Reid is old news. I have somebody new in mind."

Something the size of a basketball settled in my stomach. I thought I knew who she was talking about. I started to ask her, but the bell rang and we sprinted for class.

We had a sub in English lit and I guess the guy didn't have a lesson plan prepared. He introduced himself as Mr. Perry and then said, "What's the last book you read? We'll go around the class and answer."

I shrunk down in my chair. I hated this stuff. I liked to read, but not the kind of stuff everybody else read. It was pretty much as expected, until the end.

Bridget's was obvious. "Jennifer Aniston's biography."

"*The Joy of Sex*," Rich Edmunds said.

"Read it again," Bridget suggested. Even the sub laughed at that.

Finally, it was my turn. "*Hustler Days*." I knew everybody would get the wrong idea. Rich snickered.

Mr. Perry said, "Minnesota Fats, right?"

"You've read it?"

He said, "I played a few games when I was in college. State College has a great tournament every year."

The rest of the class looked at us like we were speaking a foreign language.

"Billiards," he explained. "Also known as pool. Great book."

I smiled at him. "I thought so, too."

The bell rang and Bridget caught up with me in the hallway. The *snap, snap, snap* of her gum was driving me crazy, but I didn't dare say anything to her when she was in a mood.

She was focused on her gum commercial. Her agent was due to call any minute and Bridget was irritable.

"What the heck were you and that nerdy sub talking about?" she said.

"A book about pool," I said.

She lost interest when she saw Alex heading our way. I met his eyes and shook my head. I needed to talk to Alex alone. He retreated. Bridget hadn't noticed my little signal, but she pouted the rest of the day because Alex hadn't rushed over.

* * *

After lunch, Kayley grabbed me. "What's going on with you and Bridget?" she said.

"Nothing," I said.

"Give me a break," she said, "the two of you were barely talking at lunch and usually we can't shut you up."

"Nothing is wrong," I said.

"Watch yourself with Bridget," she warned. "I don't want to see you get hurt."

I stared her down, despite the panic welling up inside me. "I don't know what you're talking about." Rule one. Deny, deny, deny.

"Chloe," she said. "I saw the way you looked at him. You're in pretty deep already."

My heart stopped. Kayley knew my secret. I'd trusted her with it, but if she said something to Bridget, it was over.

"Why are you being so harsh?" I said. "I know you don't like her, but please, don't say anything to Bridget, okay? I'll tell her when I'm ready."

Kayley replied, "Chloe, I'm saying this as a friend. Bridget plays for keeps and you're in over your head." Kayley walked off without a backward glance.

"What's her problem?" Bridget came up behind me. Had she heard Kayley? No sign of an imminent explosion. I was safe for now.

"I don't know. We were just talking about guys," I admitted. It wasn't exactly a lie.

"Perish the thought," Bridget said. "Whatever Kayley's advice was, don't listen to it. I mean, she's only ever dated Vinnie. She doesn't know anything about boys."

Why weren't Bridget's words more of a comfort?

I spent the rest of the day wishing there were a best friend's witness protection program, one for people who lied to their best friend.

I was glad when school was over. Thankfully, Bridget had something going on after school, so I didn't wait for her. Guilt didn't stop me from cruising through the hallways looking for Alex's locker.

I planned to casually bump into him and take it from there. But evidently, Bridget had the same idea because she was in front of his locker. She was standing close to Alex as they talked. As I approached, he ran his hand down her arm and smiled at her.

From where I stood, it looked like Bridget had Alex locked. He glanced up and saw me. Our eyes met for a brief moment before I walked away. Part of me was hoping that he'd come running after me, but he didn't.

I walked home alone, kicking myself for thinking that I could compete with Bridget.

When I got to the house, the phone was ringing. I threw my backpack on the floor and raced to answer it.

"McBride residence," I said, regretting the impulse that made me pick up right away. I didn't feel like talking to anybody.

"This is Alex," a voice said in my ear. A traitorous thrill shot through me, but I braced myself against the onslaught of his charm.

"Well, hello, Alex," I said. "It's nice to *finally* hear from you."

"Meet me at Gino's," he said persuasively. "Please."

I drew in a startled breath. "I'm busy. Permanently busy."

"Please, Chloe," he said softly, "I want to explain."

"There's nothing to explain," I said. "Bridget's my best friend. I made a mistake."

"No, you didn't," he insisted. "Give me five minutes. Is that too much to ask?"

I hung up the phone without answering, but somehow a heartbeat later, my feet carried me in the direction of Gino's.

I found Alex by the pool tables, naturally. A group of freshmen girls were checking him out. Naturally. I tried not to act as obvious as the freshmen, but he looked heart-wrenchingly handsome in a black shirt and gray chinos.

When he saw me, a smile lit up his face and he hurried over. "Chloe, you made it."

We walked back to his table and he handed

me a cue stick. "Feel like a game? I could use a challenge."

"Is that what I am? A challenge?" I said. Part of me wondered if he was interested in me only as a pool partner.

"Yes," he said. "In the best sense of the word. I've never met anyone like you, Chloe. And I want to get to know you."

I was skeptical. What was so special about me? "It looked to me like you were getting to know *Bridget*, from the way you were holding her hand."

"She was holding my hand and she didn't even do that until she saw you. Besides, I think she was trying to make her boyfriend jealous."

Had Reid been there, too? I hadn't noticed. It was all happening so fast. I couldn't think. But what could it hurt to play a game of pool? It was perfectly innocent, I told myself.

Alex touched my hair, softly stroking the strands. It gave me the shivers. "It's not like Bridget and I have been seriously going out or anything. I can't help how she feels. And I can't help the way I feel about you either. I like you, Chloe."

He reached for me, but I took a step away. "Let's play."

He grinned at me. "Sure. It'll make you feel better."

He was right. I did feel better. I felt the most like myself when I held a pool cue in my hand. With pool, I had everything under control, unlike the rest of my life. Or so I thought. But when I was with Alex, *everything* seemed out of control.

He racked the table and I broke. The ten ball spun into the center pocket. So I was stripes. I miscalculated the spin on my next shot and missed.

Then it was his turn. He was pretty good, but I managed to take the game back when he missed the two ball. I took shot after shot, not even realizing that I'd nearly cleared the table until I stopped to chalk and finally noticed Alex staring at me.

Despite the distraction of his concentrated gaze, I made my shot. He looked like he was having a good time, which was a relief. Most guys hated that I could beat them at pool.

"Where did you learn to play?" I asked after he made his shot.

"My uncle Gino taught me," he said. "What about you?"

"My Dad. And your uncle taught me to play, too." He missed his shot and came to stand next to me.

My turn. I had a hard time concentrating on the game.

I ran my hand up and down my cue. Part of winning at pool was watching your opponents. I had predicting my opponents' moves down to an art form. Nothing broke my concentration until Alex.

He stood directly behind me as I planned my shot. His soft breath warmed the nape of my neck. And he smelled so good. I could smell the spicy cologne he wore.

I stretched across the table to make a bank shot. Was he staring at my butt? I was so distracted I missed the shot.

I swore under my breath.

Alex grinned at me. "Show me that shot again," he said. And this time, I concentrated and made it.

"I think I finally have it perfected," I said.

"Yeah, I've never seen a bank shot quite like it," he said. His smile sent a shiver down my spine.

I sat on one of the tall barstools in the corner and told my horny little subconscious to mind her manners and concentrate on the game.

Then our eyes met and Alex reached over and gently took the pool cue out of my hand. I noticed how quiet it was at Gino's. It was as if we were alone.

When he leaned in, I sucked in my breath and reined in my raging hormones. Or at least I tried to, but Alex's lips were soft when they met mine.

Much, much later, I pushed him away. But it was too late. With a delayed sense of dread, I heard the sound of footsteps and the angry snap of chewing gum.

Bridget stood a few feet away.

She looked at me like she was looking at a rock, or maybe a stranger she passed on the street. But I heard the snap of her gum, the sound of her jaw as it clenched. She didn't say anything. She reached over and stroked my hair.

For a minute I thought it would be all right, that the three of us would be able to work it out. I breathed in the sweet smell of bubble gum.

Her face changed, turned pink, and then she mashed a huge wad of gum in my hair. She took her time, concentrating on doing a thorough job.

Alex made a sound of protest, but I shook my head. I didn't even try to stop her. He said something to her in a low voice. Then my former best friend burst into tears and ran out.

I didn't follow her. I knew it was too late. My best friend was gone.

Alex gave me a ride in his shiny black Mercedes. It crossed my mind that the color matched his hair exactly, something that smacked of trying too hard. I dismissed the thought as petty.

I shouldn't take my bad mood out on Alex. I wanted to kick myself. Why had I started this thing with him? I was numb, still in disbelief that Bridget had stuck gum in my hair. What was she, five?

Why couldn't things stay the same? Why did people have to change?

We didn't talk in the car, except when Alex gestured to my hair. "Do you want me to get you something for that?"

"No, take me home, please," I said wearily.

I was careful to lean away from the neck rest. I could feel the gum she'd put in my hair, right at the base of my neck.

The only time Bridget and I ever got into a fight, until now anyway, was over the stupidest thing. We were in sixth grade and it was the day we saw "the film."

At our school, we saw two sex education films, one in fifth grade and one in sixth. The fifth grade film covered the basics, but the sixth grade film got into the details about sex.

I overheard Bridget and Lia Cruz.

"Who do you think will be the last virgin in class?" Lia said.

"Boy or girl?" Bridget asked.

"Nobody *cares* when boys lose it," Lia said, "so girl, of course."

"It'll be Chloe," Bridget said immediately. I didn't know what hurt more, that she obviously thought I was so completely lacking in sex appeal or that it took her all of two seconds to come up with my name.

I didn't talk to Bridget for a whole week, which was an eon in sixth grade. Finally, she asked me what was wrong.

"I heard you," I said. "Telling Lia that you thought I'd be the last virgin in our class."

Bridget stared at me. "What's wrong with that?" she said. "I know you won't sell yourself short and give it up to the first guy who hands you a line. I meant it as a compliment."

"Really?" I said, feeling ridiculously pleased.

"Of course," she said. "You're the practical one."

But now my practical side had flown out the window. Maybe that meant that Alex was the one I'd been waiting for. I'd never acted like this before, never felt like this.

I didn't want to admit that this thing with Alex was going to be a problem, but part of me knew it was going to end badly. I couldn't seem to stay away from him.

I tortured myself by replaying the look of contempt on Bridget's face. When we pulled into my driveway, Alex gave me a quick kiss on my cheek and said good night.

I went inside. I'd seriously screwed up this time.

I went straight to bed and pulled the covers up over my head, not even bothering to change into pajamas. I was beyond tired. I'd take a look at the damage in the morning.

Chapter Ten

When I got up, my hair was a mess. The gum had hardened into some super substance. If there were a nuclear Armageddon, the only things left would be cockroaches and Bridget's gum in my hair.

My glance fell on a photo of the two of us from a couple of years ago. We were at Disneyland, wearing Mickey ears and huge smiles. I winced. We were also wearing identical Hawaiian shirts. Bridget had picked them out. She looked gorgeous. I looked anemic.

I threw a baseball cap over my hair, just in case Mom was up, then snuck downstairs and tried ice cubes to get the gum out. It didn't work.

Fortunately for me, my sister, Nina, was home for one of her rare weekend visits. I tapped softly on her door. It was almost nine. She had to be up by now.

"Nina, are you awake? Can I come in? Psst. Nina, I have a fashion emergency." That'd wake her up if anything would.

"Chloe, what do you want? The sun's barely up, but

I'm awake now. You may as well come in," She sounded half-asleep, but I was desperate.

"It's after nine, lazybones. Besides, I need your help." I took off the baseball cap I'd been wearing.

Her mouth fell open. "What happened to you?" Nina jumped out of bed. "Do we have any peanut butter?"

"You're hungry at a time like this?" I said.

"For your hair," she explained.

"It's too late," I confessed. "I slept with it in my hair."

"What happened? Never mind, you can tell me in the car." She flipped open her cell phone and punched in some numbers. After a brief, low-voiced conversation, she hung up. "Get dressed."

"Where are we going?" I said.

"To my stylist. And bring your babysitting money, because this is going to cost you a fortune," she said grimly. She shooed me out of her room to get dressed. She met me in the hallway a few minutes later, wearing sweats, her face bare. I must have been a true mess because Nina never went anywhere, not even the grocery store, without lip gloss and mascara.

We tiptoed down the stairs and left a note for my mom, who was still sleeping.

I told Nina what had happened with Bridget. I even confessed that I wore her dress without permission. I was so glad Nina was home. I missed her. Our whole family felt completely different now that it was only Mom and me.

"I'm sorry about the dress."

To my relief, she didn't lecture me. "Don't worry about the dress. It can be replaced," she said. "And you *will* replace it." She smiled to soften the words.

"Thanks for listening, Nina. I can't believe that Bridget did this, but it's like she couldn't help herself."

"You and Bridget should be able to work it out. You've been friends since kindergarten and you've never let a boy come between you before."

"But Alex is different," I said. "I'm not sure I can give him up, even for Bridget."

"Why? What's so special about this boy?"

"It's the way Bridget is acting," I explained. "Remember when we were little and we used to race to see who could eat the most cereal? So we could get to the prize at the bottom of the box?"

"God, we were so serious about that. I ate so much it hurt," Nina said. "I was determined that no matter what, I'd get that ring."

"That's exactly how it is with Bridget. Alex is like the prize at the bottom of the cereal box."

"Now you're grown up and there's a lot more at stake than a plastic ring."

"Exactly," I said, nodding.

"I don't know what you're going to do about Bridget, but don't let Mom find out," Nina said.

"If Bridget ever talks to me again," I said.

Nina gave my hand a squeeze, and then returned her attention to the road. "She will, Chloe. She's hurt. But Mom will freak out if she finds out what Bridget did to your hair."

"Yeah, Mom's been acting really overprotective lately. She drove me to Bridget's house last weekend and I swear I thought she was going to come in the house with me."

"What's with Mom's clothes?" Nina said.

"You mean her new Stepford Wife look?" I said. "I have no idea, but I miss her old look." Mom used to be a hip dresser, but lately, I'd only seen her in crisply starched khakis and button-down shirts. It was like she was trying on this new identity.

I figured it would be easier to explain after Nina's stylist fixed my hair.

Her stylist worked in an old California bungalow on Pacific Coast Highway. Like many of the old houses on PCH, it had been converted into an office building.

We found parking a block away, a minor miracle in Laguna Beach.

Terry, the stylist, took a look at my hair and shrieked. "What possessed you to leave gum in your hair all night?" he said. "Rough night?" He winked.

"You have no idea," I sighed.

"It's a shame, but all this has got to go," he said, gesturing at my long hair. "We have to cut it."

I couldn't bear to look. I squeezed my eyes shut until it was over.

"You can peek now," Terry said.

My head felt strangely light. I stared at the floor. I was too scared to see what he'd done. Terry held up a thick swath of hair and twirled it around. "It's long enough. I have to keep it in a ponytail if you want to give it to Locks of Love."

"I can't look."

"Chloe, it's gorgeous! It's the perfect cut for you." Nina said. She gave Terry a hug. "You're a genius."

I finally glanced in the mirror and ran a hand over my hair. Amazed, I checked the mirror again. I couldn't believe it was me in the mirror. My hair framed my face in soft wisps. Suddenly, my cheekbones were more pronounced and my eyes were wide and mysterious. I liked it.

I started to get out of the chair.

"Wait," Terry stopped me. "How about highlights?"

I didn't say anything. I was trying to figure out if I had enough babysitting money with me.

Nina slapped down her credit card, the one our parents had given her for emergencies. "Great. Reds and golds, I think."

I nodded and gave her a grateful smile. She was the best big sister there was. Terry and Nina looked at each other and gave each other a high five. I relaxed in the chair.

When we got back from the salon, Mom took one look at my hair and wigged out.

"What did you do to yourself?" Mom screeched.

Nina and I exchanged glances. It was a good thing she hadn't seen me before the stylist worked his magic.

"They cut off your beautiful long hair," she wailed.

Nina interrupted our semi-hysterical mother. "Mom, take a look at her. She looks great. That cut sets off her green eyes and her cheekbones. She had too much hair anyway. Let it go, already."

A warm glow spread through me. Nina was a fashion maven and wouldn't sugarcoat it. If she liked my new cut, it must be flattering.

"My hair went to a good cause. I gave it to Locks of Love," I said. The parts not covered in gum went there, anyway. "You know, the place that makes wigs for kids who've lost their hair."

After she stopped freaking out, my mom finally stopped and took a good look at me. I shifted from foot to foot. I didn't want to admit it, but I hoped she would approve of my new look.

I knew she liked it when she finally said, "How

about if we go shopping? You could use some new clothes to go with your new look. And I could use some new things as well."

Both Nina and I stared at her. It was true she could use a little shopping spree.

Maybe a shopping trip would result in her returning to her usual hip-artist-chick self.

"I'll take a rain check, Mom. I have a date tonight," Nina said.

I threw a sharp look at my sister. Nina was turning down shopping? It must be love. Or a really cute guy.

"I don't suppose you'd like to come, would you?" Mom said to me. She knew I hated shopping.

"I wanted to watch this movie tonight on television. Thanks anyway, Mom." I didn't want to run into Bridget or Alex. And I was still getting used to the strangely freeing sensation from my lack of hair. I felt bare, vulnerable.

"Maybe I'll call Karen and see if she's free. I should go change." Mom left the room humming. We stared after her.

"What's with Mom?" I said.

Nina said, "Weird, but it's about time she starting taking an interest in something again."

"I'm just happy to see her leave the house," I said.

"I should get ready myself," Nina said. "Will you be okay?"

"I'll be fine."

After Mom left, I decided it was time to deal with my personal problems. I dialed Bridget's number.

She answered on the first ring and before she could hang up, I said, "I thought we weren't going to let a guy come between us."

"So did I," she said. There was a long pause and then, "I'm sorry about putting gum in your hair. I completely lost it. I'm really sorry."

She sounded sincere, but I didn't know what to say to her. I'd never seen Bridget act like that before.

"It's okay," I said. "I had to get it cut, but it looks better short anyway."

"It does?" There was a strange note in her voice. Then she added, "I like him, you know."

"I do, too." My voice sounded high and tense.

A lengthy pause and then, "Has Alex seen it?"

"Bridget, what's going on? You sound jealous or something."

"Maybe I am," she said, and then there was a click, and that's when I realized that my best friend had hung up on me.

I went to Nina's room. She was getting ready for her hot date.

"Thanks for going with me today," I said.

"You're welcome, little sis," she said. "What are you going to do tonight?"

"Hang out," I said. "I don't need any more drama in one weekend."

"Do you want me to stay home with you?" she said.

She was a great sister, but I could tell she was hoping I'd say no. Which any decent sister would do.

I shook my head. I could handle a night on my own.

Chapter Eleven

After both Mom and Nina left, the house felt empty. Normally, Bridget would come over to keep me company. I wandered through the house, looking at all the empty spots on the wall where my father's paintings used to be. The real ones, not the phony stuff he churned out now.

I stopped in the family room. There was a new painting above the couch. It was of a gorgeous sunrise, all flaming reds and brilliant yellows. I wondered who had painted it, but as I leaned forward to see if it was signed, the doorbell rang.

I ran to answer it, hoping in vain that it was Bridget on my doorstep.

It wasn't. Alex Harris stood there with a smile on his face. He had a small bag in his hand.

"What are you doing here?" I hissed. "Get out of here before someone sees you."

"Chloe, I know you're probably mad at me," he said, "but can I come in and talk to you?"

I started to shut the door.

"I brought your dress," he said. "It's washed and everything. Doesn't that count for something?"

I softened. How many guys do laundry for you? Not many. My common sense told me to keep that door shut. He meant trouble. Obviously, I wasn't listening because I opened the door again.

"Come in," I said, "but you have ten minutes."

We stood in the foyer, awkwardly avoiding looking at each other. I couldn't help wondering if he liked Bridget more. Had he shown up to tell me that he'd decided he wanted to be with her instead of me? I repressed the thought.

Somehow, no matter how much I told myself otherwise, Bridget and I were competing for the same guy. Something we'd promised we'd never do.

"So what are you doing here? Bridget saw you first."

Alex grinned at my last sentence. "Technically, I met you first. And I'm not a pair of marked-down jeans at a sale. I have some say in it, you know. It's very simple. I want to go out with you."

"Me?" I said in disbelief. "I'm a mess." But I noticed he didn't say he *didn't* want to go out with Bridget.

"There aren't many girls like you," he said. He reached out a hand and touched my hair. "And I like your new look."

I folded my arms over my chest. I wasn't convinced. "You don't even know me."

"Sure, I do. Remember the beach?" he said. "I know you hate crowds, love pool, and think that I'm scamming you, which isn't true."

"But what about Bridget? She's not even speaking to me."

"Look, I want to get to know you, Chloe. Give me a chance. And if Bridget really is your best friend, she'll get over it." Alex seemed sincere, but how could I be sure?

"But what if she doesn't get over it? Then I've lost a friend. And I didn't even know you two were seeing each other."

He said, "I'm sorry about that. I didn't mean to come between you. How about a game of pool to make up for it? You're entering the pool tournament at Gino's, right? I know I could use a little practice."

I looked at him, startled. I hadn't even thought about it, but Alex was entering the tournament, too. It was likely I'd have to play him. Another complication I didn't need.

"There's this great place in Newport," he continued.

I nodded. Bridget wouldn't even have to know, I thought. But there wasn't going to be anything to know because I was going to keep my hands (and the rest of my various body parts) to myself.

*   *   *

The pool place was one of those trendy touristy restaurants, but the pool tables were brand-new and high quality. The felt on the tables was pristine, without beer bottle rings or cigarette burns.

At first I felt self-conscious as Alex watched my every move. He ordered some munchies while we waited. We finally got a pool table and I got over my self-consciousness as soon as I racked the table. Pretty soon, I didn't even notice him.

What I did notice was my mother as she walked in and took a seat at the bar. She hadn't looked around but made a beeline to a stool. Her back was to me. The bartender brought her a drink, one of those froufrou things you whip up in a blender and garnish with a little umbrella.

What on earth was my mother doing here? She was pretty dressed up for a night out with her friend Karen. Mom was wearing her hip-chick clothes. Faded jeans hugged her figure. My mother was also wearing my favorite halter and filled it out considerably better than I did.

A tall man with curly blond hair strode into the bar. I lost my concentration and missed my shot. Alex took the opportunity and sunk a couple of shots. Out of the corner of my eye, I noticed he was a decent player, controlled, but a little slick. But my attention kept drifting back to my mother.

I watched as my father made his way over to the bar and put his hand on my mom's shoulder. As he took a seat next to her, it dawned on me. My mother was out on a date with Devon McBride.

Alex had his phone out. He talked to someone in a low voice as I tried to make a shot. He was engrossed in his conversation and didn't notice my distraction, but my hands were shaking. I barely made the shot.

I turned away from the sight, called the eight ball, and sank it.

"Sorry about that. It was a call I had to take," Alex said. "Great game. Are you ready to eat? Let's get a table."

"Do you mind if I take a rain check?" I said. Lame, but I didn't want to watch my parents making googly eyes at each other. "I'm not feeling that great," I added.

After Alex dropped me off, I stepped inside and leaned against the front door. Real date or not, I had a great time, almost too good, until I'd spotted my parents, anyway. I thought he had fun, too.

He hadn't kissed me even though there was a moment at the restaurant when he stood so close to me that I could barely breathe. We looked into each other's eyes. But I blew it.

He leaned forward, I think to kiss me, but I almost brained him with my pool cue.

I didn't *want* Alex to kiss me anymore, right? But a sneaky thought popped into my mind. If he didn't kiss me, how was I going to know? I still wanted him to kiss me, even though I knew it would piss Bridget off.

The damage was already done with her, anyway, but she'd get over it. Why not go out with him?

I sighed and locked the front door. It was quiet, too quiet. The house was empty. It was way past time for a separated, but friendly, dinner to be over.

Saturday nights for my mom usually meant drinking a glass of white wine while she sobbed her heart out to the flicker of some old tearjerker movie.

I wandered to the front room and pulled back a curtain to peer out the window. I looked at my watch. It was almost midnight.

I heard the sound of an engine and peered out again. A car pulled up in front of the house and sat idling at the curb. It looked like the midlife crisis car my dad bought after he left us.

It was a long time before the door opened and my mother emerged. I didn't want to think about what they were doing in that car for so long.

Mom practically levitated up the front steps. I didn't want to get caught staring out the window like some overprotective mom so I scooted to the kitchen. I heard my mother's key in the lock and then her footsteps as she headed toward the kitchen.

"Hi, Mom. I'm in here," I said, trying to sound casual, even though I wanted to tie her to a chair and shine a light in her eyes until she confessed everything.

I opened the fridge and pretended to be looking for a soda. As my mother entered, I grabbed a bottle of cola and set it on the counter. I pulled a glass from the cupboard with studied nonchalance.

"Want one?" I offered my mother a glass, sneaking a peek at her when I thought she wasn't looking.

Mom was glowing, radiant, lit from within. She looked — in love. I got a sinking feeling in my stomach. Mom *could not* be dating Devon McBride.

I shuddered. I took a long sip of my soda. Yuck, generic. My mom was getting a little out of control with the budget bit.

"I wondered where you'd gone," I said.

"I went out for a bit," my mom replied.

"Where?" I said, pretending not to care, but really hanging on my mother's every word.

"With a friend." It was like pulling teeth to get an answer from her.

"You didn't leave a note," I added sternly.

"Oh, I, I forgot — something came up at the last minute. Sorry."

"What?" I said, with a sinking feeling. My mother looked happy, happier than she'd been in months. "Tell me what's going on, Mom."

My mother giggled. "No, I don't think I'll share my good news yet. I'll wait until your sister comes back. Is Nina coming home tonight or going back to the dorm? It'll have to wait until I can tell you together. In person." She left the room, still giggling softly.

"But, Mom —" Dad was definitely back.

"I'm going to bed. We'll talk more in the morning. Night, honey."

"Good night, Mom." I stared after my mother. Yep. It was love all right.

The cola tasted like acid. I hadn't even realized it until now, but I hadn't thought that it would be possible for my parents to get back together.

What were we going to do? I couldn't wait until my sister returned home to find out what was up with our mom.

But Nina had other plans and was already gone when I got up the next morning. By the time I tracked her down, she was holed up in her dorm, studying.

"Nina, are you sure you can't come back home? I know you were just here, but Mom refuses to spill her big news until she can tell us both in person."

I knew how hard my sister worked to get good grades. Nina always pulled down As. I wished that playing pool were an academic activity. Playing pool would be a guaranteed A for me. Although I didn't want to play pool forever, I didn't know what I wanted to do.

"No, I'm sorry, but I absolutely have to finish this paper. It's due on Monday. I'll be there Wednesday night at the latest, okay?"

"Okay, Nina, but please, by Wednesday, okay? Mom's acting really weird," I said.

I could tell by my sister's "uh-huh" that Nina's mind was already on her paper.

Dropping my voice in case my mom was nearby listening, I continued, "He dropped her off last night and she stayed in the car for a long time."

Nina answered with another "uh-huh," but I could hear the sound of a keyboard clicking in the background.

"Don't you care that Mom may be having an affair? With our own father?"

Her voice was sharp. "Chloe, Mom's not having an affair with Dad. She can't be. They're still married."

"Right," I said. "But that didn't stop him from disappearing for years and hurting her last time, did it?"

There was silence on the other end of the line. I finally had my sister's undivided attention.

Chapter Twelve

Nina came home on Wednesday night, like she'd promised. We had Thai takeout for dinner, and then Mom led us into the living room and made us sit down before she'd talk to us.

"First, I wanted to let you know that your father and I have been talking lately."

I gave Nina a told-you-so look. She stuck out her tongue at me.

I started to get off the couch. *That* was my mom's idea of great news, even after everything she'd been through?

But Mom surprised me.

"Now, close your eyes," she said.

Nina and I looked at each other, exasperated.

"Mom, come on!" Nina said. "I've got to get back to school."

She left the living room and came back a minute later holding a thin stack of papers held tight by a rubber band.

Nina looked as perplexed as I felt.

"I'm writing again," Mom said, "And it's the best work I've done in years." Her cheeks were pink and her eyes looked like blue stars.

Nina and I didn't know what to say. It had been so long since she'd done anything new. She removed the rubber band and handed me the manuscript.

"It's something new I'm trying," she explained. "I showed it to your father and he loved it."

Nina and I both got up from the couch to hug her. "Congratulations, Mom," Nina said. "How is Dad taking it?" There was only one star in the McBride family.

"That's the best part," she said. "He showed it to a publisher and they're interested. Your dad is so excited."

"Mom, that's wonderful!" I said. Nina and I exchanged glances. It didn't sound like the dad we knew. Mom's career always came after the great Devon McBride's.

"I have one book done," she said. She motioned to the stack. "He might even illustrate it. The publisher thought that a husband and wife team was a great idea. And your dad is going to enter his work at the festival show."

"Mom, it's great that you're writing again." I gave her a hug. "We should be celebrating your first book contract."

"Chloe's right," Nina said. "Let's go out for a decadent dessert. My treat."

"Mine, too!" I said. I could replenish the cue fund another time. I was thrilled for my mom.

She'd been hiding her light for too long, but I wondered why she'd decided to start writing again. It explained why she'd been spending so much time with Devon lately. He was helping her to get her career started again. Maybe Mom was finally getting a chance to shine.

A week went by without Bridget speaking to me. Unless you count the nonverbal message she gave me with her middle finger when I saw her in the hallway. I was going to have to talk to her soon, but I needed to find the right time. I'd been spending lunch in the library. I knew it was the last place any of my friends would look for me, but the smell of ink and paper was strangely intoxicating. I spent my lunches rereading *Hustler Days* and doing my homework.

Friday came and I still couldn't bring myself to approach her. She glared at me whenever I walked within five hundred feet.

Alex came by as I was waiting by my locker.

"Hi there, gorgeous," he said.

"Hi, yourself." I smiled up at him. He leaned over to kiss me. I looked around guiltily, but there was no sign of Bridget, so I kissed him back, leaning into him. As if the kiss had set off some sort of internal alarm, Bridget walked by a few minutes later.

"Gotta bolt," Alex said. He practically ran down the hall. I told myself he was probably late for class, but I noticed he went in the same direction as Bridget.

I tried not to worry. He couldn't be interested in Bridget if he'd kissed me like that.

I'd been hiding in the library at lunchtime to avoid Bridget, but today I was sick of eating alone.

I stood in the lunch line next to Theo.

"Hi, Chloe," Theo said. "I haven't seen you around lately." He stared at my hair, but didn't say anything.

I ran a hand over it self-consciously.

"Hey, Theo." He followed me as I filled my tray.

I spotted Bridget at the high-maintenance table with the other girls who spent all their time in tanning booths all winter and on the beach all summer. Then there were the facials, nails, eyebrows. No wonder they never ate. There wasn't enough time.

Bridget caught me staring at her. She glared at me, then bent her head and whispered something to Lia, who burst into gales of high-pitched laughter.

I winced. I imagined what Bridget was saying about me and none of it was good.

Theo said, "Ignore her. She'll get over it eventually."

But what if she didn't? I had the awful feeling that my best friend was dumping me for good. Stuff like that got around and pretty soon, everyone would be wondering what I'd done wrong. Either that, or Bridget would be telling them.

Theo steered me to a table where Vinnie and Kayley sat. Susi Samala sat on Kayley's other side.

I said hi to Susi, who I knew from Spanish class. I bit into my apple, trying to ignore the evil looks Bridget was throwing my way. I knew she was hurt, too, but she was acting really immature.

Anyone from the outside would never believe that we were best friends until a few days ago. I tried to ignore her, but there was a feeling of dread in my stomach. She was used to getting what she wanted. And she wanted Alex. The thought occurred to me that she wanted Alex more than she wanted me as a friend.

Kayley leaned around Susi to say, "I like your hair."

"Thanks."

"What made you decide to cut it?" Theo said.

"I — I wanted a change," I said. I didn't know what to say. There was no way I was going to tell them the truth, at least not in front of Susi. I didn't know her well enough to talk about my humiliating little love triangle.

Theo frowned. He bit into an apple thoughtfully. "I liked your hair long," he said mulishly. "You don't need to change to impress anybody."

I stared at him until he met my eyes. "I'm not."

"Well, I like it," Kayley said. "Chloe, do you want to meet at Gino's after school to practice? The tournament isn't far off."

"Sure," I said.

"I'll see you there then." I smiled at her. I knew she was trying to distract me from Bridget's bitchiness, but it wasn't really working.

For the first time, Bridget saw me as competition, which meant Bridget didn't want anything to do with me. It dawned on me that when Bridget did hang around me it was because she didn't see me as competition.

"I heard Alex Harris is entering, too. He'll be tough to beat, right, Theo?" Kayley continued.

Theo, who had a mouth full of sandwich, simply nodded.

They were all looking at me. I shrugged, "What's the big deal if we have to play against each other?"

Kayley rolled her eyes. "What's the big deal?" she said.

I stopped chewing and glanced at her inquiringly.

"The big deal is that guys don't like to lose to their girlfriends, that's what the big deal is."

"She's not his girlfriend," Theo said. His hazel eyes gleamed green. "Are you?"

"I'm not his girlfriend," I said, "but we have gone out a couple of times."

Theo grunted and resumed chewing. A few minutes later, he asked, a shade too casually, "Did you get your dress back okay?"

There was something about the expectant tone in his voice that gave me a clue. "Theo," I said, "did you wash it for me?"

He said, "Sure. It was the least I could do after being so clumsy. I asked Alex to give it to you . . ." His voice trailed off.

Kayley and I looked at each other. She seemed to be trying to tell me something with that look, but what?

I was trying to recall Alex's exact words. He hadn't *said* he'd washed the dress, but he'd certainly implied it, hadn't he? Now I wasn't sure.

I didn't feel like eating any longer and gave Theo my dessert. I knew he had a sweet tooth.

After school, I headed to Gino's. I needed to practice, and now that Bridget wasn't speaking to me, I didn't have anything else to do.

I needed to think about how to fix Bridget and me and I thought best with a stick in my hand. There had to be a solution to our problem, one that didn't mean me giving in and giving up Alex.

If only he'd choose between us. But I wasn't ready to ask him to choose. I was afraid he wouldn't pick me. He hadn't made a decision yet. I had a niggling feeling that Bridget was still in the running.

When I walked into Gino's, Kayley was already at a table. She looked up from her game. "Ready to play? I could use the practice."

"Me, too." I hated to admit it. "The tournament's coming up soon and I haven't had enough time to practice."

She said, "I'll rack. What do you want to play?"

"What category are you playing in the tournament?" I asked.

"I'm not," she said. "I thought you might want someone to practice with."

I smiled at her. "Thanks, Kayley. Eight ball it is."

I grabbed the rack and lined up the number one through nine balls.

"Trash counts," she said.

"Of course," I replied.

Kayley took the break and sent the number one ball spinning into the side pocket. She missed the next shot, but gave me a "what can you do" shrug.

I chalked my cue.

She said, "Got a sponsor yet?"

I shook my head. I said, "If I were speaking to my father, I might even ask him."

She hesitated. "Why aren't you speaking to him?"

"It's complicated. They're separated, but just when I was getting used to the idea of a divorce, he's hanging around again. It pisses the hell out of me, but part of me wants him back home."

"And the other part?" she said.

"The other part wishes he'd leave us alone."

I took a deep breath and aimed for the two ball. It needed a kiss to sink it. I made the shot.

I was having fun. Kayley understood that conversation had to stop when I was concentrating on a shot, which was something Bridget never got. Kayley was a good player, steady and committed. Once she decided on a shot, she followed through, no matter what.

We were down to the eight ball and it was my turn. I sunk it in one clean shot.

"Good game," I said. "If you practiced more, you could be really good."

"Thanks, but it's not really my thing," Kayley said. "It was fun though. Want to go get some coffee?"

I smiled. "I'd love to."

As we walked along, I told her about what really happened to my hair. I knew Kayley could keep a secret.

I'd always kept her at a bit of a distance. I didn't want to admit it, but it was because she and Bridget didn't get along. Now I trusted Kayley more than I did my best friend. What did that say about Bridget and me?

Chapter Thirteen

The next morning, when I went downstairs, Alex was sitting at the kitchen table. Why was Alex Harris sitting at my kitchen table?

And even more embarrassing, my parents were sitting there with him. It was stomach-churningly obvious that my dad had spent the night.

"It's about time you woke up, sleepyhead," my dad said, a touch too heartily.

He was acting like he tucked me in every night.

I was wearing a T-shirt and raggedy old pajama bottoms. Thankfully, I'd brushed my teeth. Alex looked perfectly polished, as usual, in khakis and a crisp button-down shirt that matched his eyes.

I narrowed my eyes at him. "Don't you look preppy today."

"Ignore her," my dad said. "She's always a grump in the morning."

"What's up?" I said.

"Nothing," he said. "I just wanted to talk to you about the tournament."

"I'm looking forward to kicking your ass," I said, jokingly. I smiled at him, but he didn't smile back. *It was a joke.*

"Let's go into the living room." Alex followed me, but as soon as we were out of sight, he grabbed me and gave me a long kiss.

"You wanted to talk about the tournament?" I reminded him, suddenly in a much better mood and really glad I'd brushed my teeth before I came downstairs.

"I just wanted to make sure it wasn't going to be a problem when I win."

"You mean, when *I* win the tournament? Why should it be a problem?" I grinned at him, but his expression didn't change.

"It's just feels weird," he said. "I don't want it to come between us. Maybe one of us should withdraw." The words hung in the air.

I was shocked. "You mean me? You want me to withdraw from the tournament?"

He didn't answer, but his expression said it all.

"I'm not going to withdraw, Alex," I said.

"If I could win that tournament, maybe my uncle would . . ."

"Would what?"

"Never mind," he said.

"If you want to impress him, be prepared to play me," I said. I didn't want to sound like I was bragging, but I knew I was good. "I have a good chance of winning. Winning won't change anything between us for me, but will it for you?"

There was a long pause. "No, of course not." He didn't sound convinced.

"Good." I smiled at him. "Do you want to stay for breakfast?"

We went back into the kitchen, where my parents were standing entirely too close together. I wanted to gag when my parents announced they were making "McBride Family Blueberry Pancakes."

My dad said, "I used to make them on special occasions. Our two girls love them, don't they, Susan?"

Ha! How would he know what we like anymore? Like he's ever home on Sunday, or any other day for that matter. My parents seemed to have forgotten that they were headed for divorce court.

"Nina's not here," I said shortly. "I'm going to get dressed."

I went upstairs and called Nina at the dorm.

"He's here," I said.

"Who's there?" she said. She sounded half-asleep.

"Dad," I said. "And I think he spent the night."

"Ew. Chloe, don't talk about stuff like that before I've had my coffee," Nina replied.

"What are we going to do about it?"

"There's nothing we can do. Mom's a grown woman."

"Well, she's not acting like one."

"Listen, I've got to go, but I'll call you on your birthday, okay?"

My seventeenth birthday was almost two weeks away. I wasn't sure I'd survive my parents' reunion without Nina.

When I came back downstairs, my parents and Alex were sitting at the kitchen table with big plates of pancakes in front of them.

I stood out of view and listened in on the conversation. I wanted to hear what they were saying about me. To my disappointment, I wasn't the subject of their conversation.

"You'll love the club," I heard my dad say. "We'll have lunch and get to know each other."

My dad was taking Alex to the club? And what self-respecting "artist" belonged to a country club anyway?

"That's great," I said, walking into the kitchen. Neither of them noticed the sarcasm in my voice. They were too busy enjoying their mutual admiration society.

Dad cleared his throat. "Chloe, your mom mentioned that she hasn't seen Bridget around here lately." He always knew the exactly wrong thing to say.

Alex and I looked at each other, neither one of us saying a word. Finally, I mumbled, "Bridget's mad at me."

"Well, I'm sure whatever snit you two are in," Dad said, "you'll soon work it out."

"Devon, sometimes friends drift away," Mom said. "The girls have developed their own interests now."

"But you've been friends since kindergarten. It seems to me that's a friendship worth working out."

I hated to admit it, but he actually had a point.

I decided I'd talk to Bridget as soon as possible. Alex schmoozed with my dad for another half hour, gave me a quick kiss on the cheek, and took off.

It was only after he left that I realized he hadn't told me the real reason why he came to see me bright and early on a Sunday morning. I dismissed the thought that maybe it wasn't me he came to see.

My parents were in the family room reading the paper. My mom was sitting in my dad's lap. Ew.

"I'm going to Bridget's," I yelled, backing out of the room.

"Chloe, come in here a minute," my dad called, stopping me in my tracks.

I loitered in the doorway. "Did you want something, Dad?"

"Just to tell you how much I like Alex. Nice boy."

My mother nodded. "He seems very nice."

"That's why I'm going to sponsor him in the tournament," my dad announced.

"You're what?" I said.

"I'm sponsoring him in the tournament," my dad repeated. "I thought you'd be pleased."

"Pleased? Pleased that my own father is sponsoring some guy in the tournament that I'm playing in?" I tried to control my voice, but I could hear it shaking.

"You're playing in the tournament? I had no idea," my father said.

"That's because you didn't ask," I said. I snatched up my house keys and left. On the way, I practiced what I would say to Bridget. It was a beautiful day, sunny and clear. A good omen, I thought.

I thought wrong. When I rang the doorbell, Bridget answered right away.

"What do you want?" she said shortly.

"I wanted to talk to you about Alex," I said. "I don't want him to come between us. I had no idea —"

"Save it," she snapped. "If you think for one minute that Alex chose you over me, you're crazy."

I stared at her. "You never thought I'd be able to get a boy that you wanted," I said slowly, realizing for the first time that it was true. "That's why we've stayed friends for this long."

"He'll run back to me as soon as he gets what he wants from you. And don't flatter yourself that it's your body he's after."

I stood there, stunned by the venom in her voice. This person had been my best friend? I'd made a mistake, I knew, but I never thought that Bridget would be so cruel.

"What's that supposed to mean?"

Bridget sneered. "Did you ever think about why he chose you, Chloe? Alex is ambitious. He always gets what he wants. He didn't want you. He wanted a few pointers for the tournament. No pool tournament, no Chloe."

"You're lying," I said. I felt sick to my stomach when I remembered the conversation in the kitchen.

"He was sizing up the competition," she added. "But what do you have to offer a guy like Alex, besides a few pool moves?"

Tears welled in my eyes. I tried to hide my hurt expression, but Bridget saw it.

"Don't be surprised when your phone stops ringing," she said. "I've already won. You just won't admit it." And then she slammed the door in my face.

I walked home. I was angry that she'd made me cry. It wasn't supposed to be like this. Bridget and I had said we'd be friends forever, that nothing would come between us. But someone had. Had we ever truly been friends?

I called Alex, but he wasn't answering his cell. I hung up without leaving a message. I tried convincing myself that none of it was true, that Bridget was jealous. Alex would call me again, I told myself.

But what made me think that someone like Alex would choose me over Bridget? When I calmed down, I realized that Bridget hadn't won, at least not yet. Otherwise, she wouldn't have been such a bitch.

A few days later, all my doubts had drifted away. Alex had left me a voice mail that we were going to go out later in the week. Bridget was wrong. He wasn't using me.

I flitted around the house, singing along to my iPod at the top of my voice.

"Chloe, what's that unusual sound?" Mom peered up the stairs at me. She was grinning.

"What do you mean?" I didn't get it for a minute.

"I was teasing you. You sounded happy, honey. It's nice to see you in such a good mood," she said.

I thought about it for a minute. "I am in a good mood." I grinned back at her. It was the first time in a long time that I hadn't started the day feeling like my life was a complete disaster. For a change, my mother even made breakfast—the normal kind, not the science-experiment-gone-bad kind.

My good mood didn't make it past lunch. Bridget saw to that.

I was at our usual table with Kayley and Theo. But for some reason, Bridget slid into the seat next to me.

When she threw something my way, I thought that maybe she'd remembered my birthday. I knew it was a tabloid even before she opened her mouth. They used cheap paper.

It was our local society page/gossip rag, *The Orange*, and my dad was on the cover.

"So, McBride, your dad forgot to mention something. Like his wife and two daughters. I guess he forgot, huh?"

I always wondered what they meant by the phrase "saw red," but now I know. I couldn't even see Bridget for the film of red that clouded my vision. I wanted to slap her. So I did. Or I would have if Theo hadn't grabbed my hand and tugged it down.

"Gee, Bridget," Kayley said, deceptive and sweet, "I didn't know."

"Know what?" Bridget said.

"That you could read," Kayley said with a smirk. It's an old joke, I know, but Bridget fell for it. I couldn't help it. I started laughing. The look on her face was too priceless. She stomped off, leaving the paper. I slowly opened it.

"Don't read that, Chloe," Kayley urged. "You know they make up most of it anyway."

*　　*　　*

I moved through the week like a zombie. Between the thing with Bridget and Alex and the thing with my parents, I was a wreck. I didn't know what I wanted anymore. Except sleep. I wanted a lot of sleep.

It didn't help that I caught a glimpse of Alex in the hallway. He was at Bridget's locker and they looked like they were in the middle of an intense conversation. I hurried down the hall before either of them saw me.

I tried not to let it get to me, but the sight of them together disturbed me. It wasn't like I didn't know he was still seeing her. But I was still shaken by the way he'd been leaning into her, like the sight of her wasn't enough, like he needed to feel her skin against his.

They had acting and good looks in common. Maybe that's all it took. That night, I couldn't get the picture of Alex's hands roaming all over Bridget's perfect ass out of my head.

Chapter Fourteen

I rolled over, looked at the clock, and groaned. I had barely enough time to take a quick shower before school. Then I remembered it was the weekend and collapsed back into bed.

"Chloe, are you awake? Your dad is here." My mom's voice floated down the hall to my room.

I bolted awake. What was my dad doing here again? I sniffed the air. It smelled like — Dad's blueberry pancakes. I groaned. Not again.

I threw on some sweats and turned on my computer. There was a message from Alex. "Miss your beautiful face. I'm swamped with auditions this week, but I'll call you soon."

He was the first person who ever described me as beautiful, but I felt a twinge when I read about his auditions. Acting was another thing he had in common with Bridget.

Pissed off at my dad or not, his pancakes were to die for, so I clicked off my computer and headed downstairs. I stopped in the middle of the stairs. My dad only made pancakes on special occasions. What was he up to?

I walked into the kitchen. There he stood in front of the stove, spatula in hand, flipping pancakes onto a plate.

"Where did Mom go?" I asked and sat at the counter. My dad placed a full plate in front of me and I inhaled the smell of fresh blueberries. What was the occasion?

"To change. We're going running," he said.

I stared at him. "What are you doing?"

"Making breakfast," he said, as if he cooked blueberry pancakes every Sunday. Which he had until he'd decided to leave.

"No, why are you here?" I couldn't keep the bitterness from my voice, not that I really tried.

He said, "I live here."

"Not anymore. You moved out, remember?" It was an accusation.

"Just until your mother and I worked a few things out." His voice was less than patient.

"What do you have to work out? The divorce settlement?" I was ready to cry.

"Nobody is talking about divorce." Dad's voice was even, but I could see it took an effort for him to control it.

I pushed the pancakes aside and stood. "I've got to go. Kayley and I have plans." We would as soon as I called her.

"But you haven't eaten your pancakes. Blueberry's your favorite." He held up the plate for evidence.

"*Was* my favorite. Besides, I've got to get ready."

"Chloe, do me a favor, okay? I know I've screwed up lately, but can you trust me? It's not what it looks like."

"Yeah. Nothing ever is." And I left without answering my father's question. But I wouldn't tell Mom about the nonmention of us in the article. I wasn't going to do his dirty work for him.

I went into my room. My stomach growled. I told it to be still, I wouldn't eat something that man had cooked for me. I couldn't be bribed with a few measly blueberry pancakes by a dad who decided to make occasional appearances. I fought back tears. I had really believed my dad loved me, loved Nina, and most of all loved our mother, but I was wrong. I thought I knew him. A year ago, I would have staked my life on it.

He'd been acting like an idiot ever since he became famous.

I needed to get out of the house. I wanted to practice for the tournament. In fact, I'd try to stay out of the house all day. I picked up the phone and gave Kayley a call.

"We'll swing by and pick you up," she said. "Feel like going to shoot pool at this place in Newport?"

"Sure, but are they open this early?" I didn't really care. Any excuse would do. I needed to think about

129

what Alex had said. I still couldn't believe that he had asked me to drop out of the tournament. I couldn't believe that he was the kind of guy who couldn't take any competition from a girl.

It was starting to look like Alex Harris wasn't the right guy for me, after all.

"Chloe, are you listening?"

"I'm sorry. I spaced out for a minute. What did you say?"

"If they're not open, we'll hang out at the beach or something. Have you looked out your window? It's gorgeous out."

After I hung up, I wandered downstairs. There was no sign of my parents, so I scribbled a note and stuck it on the fridge.

The doorbell rang and when I opened it, Theo stood there, wearing his usual T-shirt and board shorts. Rain or shine, he always dressed for the beach.

"Ready to go?"

"You're coming with us?" I asked. It sounded abrupt, so I softened my tone. "I mean, I didn't even know you played anymore." What else didn't I know about Theo? Evidently, quite a lot.

Theo stood there, shifting his weight from foot to foot. "Yeah, I still play. Not often enough, but when Vinnie called, I thought it sounded like fun. We're going to this place I know."

His eyes were this incredibly clear green. I'd never noticed before. Theo usually hid behind dark glasses.

"Like a Dave & Buster's or something?"

"Not exactly," Theo said. "It's kind of a dive, but they have great tables."

Kayley and Vinnie were in the back of Theo's Jeep. Theo opened the door for me and we took off.

Theo turned onto Pacific Coast Highway and headed north to Newport. It was a gorgeous drive. It had rained the night before and the sky looked like it had been freshly washed and hung out to dry in the warm sun.

"Why don't you pick something to listen to?" Theo said. "There are some CDs in the case."

A few minutes later, we pulled into a nondescript strip mall on the fringe of Newport.

Theo gallantly opened the door for me. He had nice manners, but didn't make a big deal about it. Vinnie gave Kayley a hand getting out of the back and then pulled her into his arms for a kiss. Theo and I both looked the other way.

We walked up to the pool place. It was small and dark, between a Japanese restaurant and a dry cleaner's. A neon COLD BEER sign was missing the letter B.

I peered in through the glass door. It was dark, the kind of dark that had never been touched by sunlight. A guy dressed in black jeans and a black cowboy shirt stumbled out. He squinted against the glare of the sun. He passed us and the smell of beer came off him in waves.

"It's okay," Theo whispered as he opened the door for Kayley and me. "I play here all the time. They don't care as long as you're eighteen." I was almost seventeen and with my new hairstyle, courtesy of Bridget's bubble gum, I looked older. Eighteen, even.

A guy stood in the doorway, blocking our entrance. "No minors," he said.

"We're eighteen," Theo said. He was stretching the truth. Vinnie and Theo were eighteen and seniors. Kayley and I were lowly juniors.

"Got any ID?" The guy said it like he already knew the answer.

"I didn't bring mine," I said lamely.

"Then get out of here," he said and shut the door in our faces.

Theo looked dejected as we left.

"Theo, it's not your fault. That guy's a Neanderthal." I looked at my watch. It was still early. "Let's get out of here. Why don't we go to Balboa?"

"We could all use some sun," Theo said.

"Or we'll turn out as pasty as the guy we saw earlier," I added.

We piled back into the Jeep and headed to Balboa. Once there, we tried to figure out what to do next. "I have a volleyball in the Jeep," Theo said. "We could get in a game."

"You just happen to have a volleyball with you?" I said, feigning shock. Theo grinned at me and then jogged off.

When he came back, he was twirling the ball on one finger. "Show-off," I said, and grabbed it from him. I raced off toward the beach, Theo right behind me.

Kayley and I teamed up, which left Vinnie and Theo as our opponents.

"Losers buy lunch," I shouted.

"Pretty confident for a girl who hasn't played in years," Theo replied. "Unless you're secretly just dying to feed me. But okay, two out of three, okay?"

I nodded. He took off his shirt and I caught my breath.

He tossed me the ball. "First serve is yours."

It might be harder to win than I'd anticipated considering I was concentrating on his chest instead of the game.

I went to the line and flubbed my first serve, but by the end of the second game, we were tied up.

Vinnie grinned over the net at Kayley. "Where you taking me, babe?"

She grinned back. "You mean, where are you taking me? This game isn't over yet."

As he dove for a ball, I noticed a girl in a totally tacky thong bikini was checking out Theo. The ball went over to our side and I dove for it, a second too late.

We lost by one point, but I had to admit it was worth it just to watch Theo play.

I don't know what made me do it, but I linked arms with him as we walked off the court.

Theo's arm stiffened under mine and then he gave me a look that made me blush. He cleared his throat. "So where do you guys want to eat?"

We decided to eat at this little seafood place on Balboa peninsula. The doors were opening when we got there, and the smell of baking bread and frying seafood made my stomach growl. They seated us at a table right away.

I bit into a piece of calamari. "Tentacles, my favorite," I said, through a mouthful of food.

Theo said, "Here, have mine."

Kayley nudged me under the table, but I didn't need anyone to point out how sweet Theo was. I was having a hard time remembering why I didn't want to go out with him.

After lunch, we stopped at one of the shops with a huge banana sign on the roof. We bought Balboa Bars, vanilla ice cream dipped in chocolate. Kayley ordered crushed Oreos on hers, I chose sweet toffee, and Theo got a toothachingly sweet combo of Oreo bits and chocolate sprinkles.

"We're going to take a walk," Kayley said. Then she winked at me when Theo wasn't looking. I made a face at her before she and Vinnie wandered off toward the arcade. Then Theo and I were alone.

We sat on a bench and ate our treats. Theo had a smudge of chocolate on the corner of his mouth. I wanted to lick the chocolate away. I repressed the impulse and handed him a napkin.

I was hyper-aware of his arm, which was casually draped over the back of the bench. His fingers grazed the nape of my neck.

"I miss it," he said. "Your hair, I mean. Remember those long braids of yours?"

"Back in sixth grade," I said. "That was a long time ago."

"I still remember," Theo said.

And then I remembered, too. I finally remembered what I could have lost while I was off chasing Alex. I could have lost Theo. The knowledge overwhelmed me for a moment.

"I kind of cut my hair accidentally," I finally said.

"How do you accidentally cut your hair?" he said, teasingly.

"It's a long story," I said, but somehow I found myself telling him most of the story. I left out the part where Alex and I were kissing when Bridget saw us.

Theo didn't comment, but I could tell he knew there was more to the story.

"How's volleyball?" I asked, changing the subject. Theo played on the high school team and on a club team, too. I told myself that was why I hadn't seen much of him lately, but in reality, I wondered if Lia Cruz was occupying his time.

"Good," he said. "It's taking up a lot of time this year." *Yes! Yay, volleyball. That way, he'd be too busy to fall for Lia.*

"I kind of miss volleyball," I admitted. I'd played for a few years, but I was nowhere near as good as Theo.

"Why don't you try out?" he said. "The team could use a little fresh blood."

"Looks like you've been doing the bleeding." I touched a fresh scab on his knee. Part of me wanted to keep my hand there, but I jerked it away.

Theo wouldn't worry about competing with a girl. I'd been ignoring someone right in front of me all this time, pretending that Alex was someone he wasn't.

Vinnie and Kayley came back about an hour later. A breeze had kicked up as the sun was going down.

"Can we stay a little while longer?" I pleaded. "I want to watch the sunset."

Kayley was smothering yawns behind her hand. Even though I tried to ignore it, it was finally time to go.

We were quiet on the way home, but it had been a good day. Theo turned on the radio and we sang along to every song, even the sappy love songs.

Chapter Fifteen

Kayley caught up with me on Monday after school. "So it's your birthday on Thursday," she said cheerfully.

"Shh, don't remind me," I said. I wasn't looking forward to my birthday this year. Bridget was still pissed off at me and things were weird with Alex. He was doing a very good impression of avoiding me. In fact, things were weird all around.

"Your mom called," she said. "Friday night at Gino's, right?"

"Yeah," I said slowly, "right."

"Oh, crap," Kayley said. "It was supposed to be a surprise!"

"I'm glad you warned, er, told me," I said. My mom was planning a party for my seventeenth birthday, a little something that she'd neglected to mention to me.

I waited all week, but my mother never said a word about the party, although there were a few broad hints and whispered phone conversations. It was going to be the dreaded surprise party, then. I wondered exactly what kind of surprises were in store for me.

On Thursday, I had a few hours to kill at home before dinner and was trying to figure out if I should go to Gino's to get in a little more practice when my dad knocked on my door.

"I have something for you," he said.

"Dad," I said. "You don't have to give me anything. Honestly."

"I know I haven't been spending much time with you," he said. "And I wanted to say I was sorry. I should have asked you before I agreed to sponsor Alex." He handed me a box wrapped in green paper. My mouth went dry when I saw its long, narrow shape. I tore off the wrapping. Nestled in the box like a perfect jewel was a Fury cue stick.

Tears welled in my eyes. "Thanks," I choked out.

"Is it the right one?" Dad said anxiously. "There's something else, too." He gestured to another box, which I hadn't noticed before. When I opened it, it contained a black leather carrying case.

I hugged him. "It's perfect." It wasn't about the pool cue. It was that my dad was trying, really trying, to make us a family again.

My actual birthday was just a quiet night at home. Nina came home from school and Dad even showed up, but Bridget didn't call to say happy birthday, which was a first. In the past, she'd called on my birthday no matter how mad she'd been at me.

On Friday, I came to school to find an elaborately decorated locker, with happy birthday balloons and streamers crammed into every available space. There was a single white rose stuck through the slats.

Kayley's handiwork, I was sure.

I caught up with her before English. "Thanks for the balloons. And the rose," I added.

"I didn't give you any flowers," she said. "You must have a secret admirer. Who knows it's your birthday?"

I nudged her gently. "Everybody who walked by my locker."

She snickered. "True. Who do you think it is?" She looked at me intently.

I thought about it for a minute. "Maybe Alex, but a red rose is more his style. Maybe Theo?"

She grinned. "The girl isn't completely clueless."

I made a face at her.

"Hey," she said as the bell rang. "I'm supposed to keep you out of the way for a few hours after school. Want to come over?"

"Sure," I said. "Far be it for me to stand in the way of a truly good 'surprise.'" I made air quotes with my hands.

I hurried to class, but with a smile on my face. Theo had remembered my birthday.

Mom was waiting for me when I got home that evening. I'd been hanging out at Kayley's, so it was already after five when I walked through the door.

"It's about time," Mom said.

I said, "I told you I was going to Kayley's after school." I didn't think the "surprise" party would start so early, but Mom was already dressed and ready to go.

She had on makeup and her dark hair was freshly curled. She wore a bright blue tunic that matched her eyes and snug jeans. She was wearing the diamond drop earrings Dad gave her for their wedding anniversary a few years ago. She looked fabulous.

"We're having dinner with your father tonight," Mom said, as I threw my backpack down.

My father? Now that WAS a surprise.

"But he was just here last night. And it's Friday night!" I protested. "Maybe I have a date."

"Do you?" Mom replied calmly.

"No, but—" I started to say, but she interrupted me.

"Your dad has planned this whole night. He's even taking us to your favorite restaurant."

"Where is he taking us?" I said, not sure that my dad even remembered my favorite places anymore.

"Gino's, of course," Mom replied. "We're meeting your dad and Nina there." Mom let me drive, and I even found a parking spot only a block away.

As we walked up to the restaurant, we met Nina. I peered in the large window and saw that my father was already there, standing at the register, talking to Gino.

"Surprise," Nina said and smiled weakly.

"It was Dad's idea," she whispered as we slid into a booth.

My father came over to greet us, like we were his long-lost daughters, which I guess we were. He gave Nina a hug, which she seemed to accept with good grace, although I noticed her shoulders stiffened at his touch. Nina was mad at him, too, but she was better at hiding it than I was. My mouth went dry as my father approached.

"Happy birthday, baby. Come give your dad a hug," he said. His arms circled me and I felt like crying, wanting to sink into his comforting embrace. Instead, I stepped away from him, avoiding all but the minimum contact.

Theo, Vinnie, and Kayley all walked into the restaurant, carrying gifts. But the biggest surprise was when Lia and Bridget walked in. Bridget carried a small, brightly colored bag. I wondered if arsenic came gift wrapped.

"He invited *all* your friends," Nina said. "Even your ex-friend."

My well-meaning but clueless dad had invited my former best friend to my surprise birthday party.

Bridget looked even more amazing than usual. Her blonde hair looked freshly highlighted and she wore a notice-me red mini.

Kayley came over to give me a hug and whispered in my ear, "What is Bridget doing here?"

"I have no idea," I whispered back, "but she's up to something."

But the party really got started when Alex walked in. I hadn't spoken to him in a few days.

My father was his usual charming self, suggesting his favorites to Alex and ordering a shake for me. I stared at him. We ordered and sat around talking while we waited for our food.

"Theo, it's nice to see you," Dad said. "How's your mom?"

"Great, Mr. McBride," Theo said. "She's been gloating that she invested in a McBride, some of your earlier work."

What he didn't say is that Theo's mom was glad that she'd bought my dad's work when it was truly artistic, before he became a hack.

It made me uneasy that Bridget was there. She had managed to snag the chair opposite Alex. It wasn't much comfort that I was sitting next to him, not when he had the vision that was Bridget to look at while we ate. I took comfort that Theo was on my other side. I had someone to turn to if I needed him.

What was she up to? At first, I had hoped that she was there to make up, but she glared at me when nobody was watching.

"Chloe, you look gorgeous tonight," Alex leaned over to me and said in a low, intimate voice.

Bridget glared at me again, but when Alex turned to say something to her, she was all smiles.

What was he up to now? He'd made it pretty clear that we were over. We'd only gone out a few times, if you called shooting a couple of games of pool and rolling around in the sand going out. Was he worth losing my best friend over? I finally figured out the answer was no, but it was too late.

My dad had ordered enough food to feed the city of Laguna Beach. I had lasagna and so did Kayley.

"Want a bite of my pizza?" Lia said to Theo. She was sitting on his other side, so close that it looked like she'd been surgically attached.

"No, thanks," Theo said. He looked at me. "Want to try my ravioli?"

"Yes, please," I said. He fed me a couple of bites while Lia sat there and steamed.

"Want to play a game?" Theo said, motioning toward a table. Before I could respond, Lia stood up. "I'd love to," she said.

Theo sent me an apologetic look, but I shrugged. I should have been concentrating on Alex, but I couldn't help watching as Lia giggled and flirted her way through the game.

My dad noticed I was staring. "Don't worry," he said. "I don't think he's interested in her."

"I'm not worried." I narrowed my eyes, daring him to say anything else.

He didn't say a word, but sent me a smile. The smile that never failed to charm. It wasn't going to work this time, I told myself sourly. I wasn't quite ready to forgive him for the way he'd treated us.

"Did you know that this is where Chloe learned to play pool?" Dad said. "I taught her when she was little. We used to come here all the time." He turned to me. "Do you remember?"

"Of course I remember, Dad," I said. My dad was a patient teacher. I'd stand on a chair to reach the table. "We used to play pool every Saturday, so Mom could write."

I noticed sourly that Theo and Lia had *finally* returned to the table.

My dad tapped on his water glass. "Now, a toast to the birthday girl," he said. "And then presents."

We all raised our glasses and dutifully toasted. My dad handed me a small, brightly wrapped gift. I recognized my mother's handmade wrapping paper. They were in on this together, whatever it was.

I looked at him in confusion. "You guys already gave me a present. My new stick. A Fury," I added to Kayley.

I opened the box and gasped. Keys. Car keys.

"A car?" I shrieked.

My mother nodded. She didn't look entirely happy.

"Thanks, Mom! Thanks, Dad!" I said. "Can I see it?"

"It's outside." My dad beamed at me.

I jumped up and ran out to the parking lot, my family and friends following behind.

My dad took my hand and led me to a brand-new baby blue VW convertible.

"Do you like it?" he said.

"Oh, yes!" I said excitedly. "And I love the color."

"The color matches your eyes," Alex said.

I wanted to glare at him, but Theo was doing it for me, so instead, I smiled sweetly.

The car was blue. Bridget's eyes were blue. My eyes were not blue. My euphoria deflated. My mother frowned, but didn't say anything.

"My eyes are green," I said to him quietly.

He looked taken aback for a moment. "Not always," he said huskily. He tipped my face up and looked into my eyes. "They're not green now."

I felt the blush creeping up my face. Did my eyes really turn blue? And why was Alex flirting with me in front of Bridget? Did he have a death wish?

Theo cleared his throat and I turned away from Alex.

"Mom and Dad, it's too much," I said. I wondered what Nina would think. Her car was three years old and she'd paid for part of it herself. But I was relieved to see she was smiling.

"Happy birthday, Chloe," she said.

"Let's go back inside and cut your birthday cake," my dad said.

We trooped back inside, where there was a huge chocolate cake baked by Lucinda, one of Mom's friends, who taught at the Laguna Culinary Arts cooking school. Everyone gathered around and sang happy birthday and then we cut the cake.

I leaned over to Nina, who was sitting across from me.

"Don't you think it's weird?" I asked in a low voice, motioning to our parents with a subtle jerk of my chin. They were sitting together, heads close. They seemed oblivious to everyone around them.

My mother chattered with my father, beaming at him as she absorbed every word. She hadn't looked so happy in a long time. Their hands were entwined and they didn't seem to notice there was anyone else in the room. I looked away, feeling like I'd intruded on a private moment.

That's when I realized that both Alex and Bridget were missing. She was *not* scamming on Alex at my birthday party, was she?

I wanted to cause a scene. Fortunately, my survival instinct kicked in. I'd practically handed him to

Bridget. I had no right to be jealous. Besides, Alex's interest had cooled considerably since I refused to withdraw from the tournament.

I scanned the room. As suspected, Bridget and Alex were in the corner by the pinball machines. They were intent, eyes locked, their bodies practically touching. I narrowed my eyes. I was getting a distinct whiff of rat bastard and it seemed to be coming from him.

The rat bastard diagnosis was confirmed when Bridget wrapped herself around him like a girl burrito.

She whispered something in his ear. It took me long enough, but I finally figured out that there wasn't anything wrong with me. Alex liked playing games. He liked to pretend he was someone he wasn't; he liked to fool people into believing that there was more to him than there was. But he was just a pretty shell.

I didn't feel like fighting over Alex tonight.

"Theo, could you take me home?" I said.

Theo said, "S-sure, Chloe. Let me say good-bye to your parents first."

Bridget's head snapped up and she arched a brow, but she didn't say anything. She probably didn't want to fight in front of Alex. But I could tell she did want to fight. I couldn't deal with her at that moment. I wanted to get out of there.

I nodded, not trusting myself to speak.

"Will you drive?" My hands were shaking so badly that I knew I'd never be able to steer. I handed the keys to my new car over to him.

"Chloe, but don't you want to . . ." His voice trailed off when he saw my face.

I stared out the window. I was so angry, I felt like punching someone.

Theo cleared his throat. "So, you signed up for the tournament?" he said. "I knew you were a good player, but you've gotten a lot better since the last time we played."

"Thanks." There was silence in the car, and the tension between my shoulders eased.

Theo leaned in a little. My pulse sped up. Was he going to kiss me? Instead he cleared his throat again and said, "Weird about your parents, huh?"

"That about covers it." I shuddered.

He said, "Do you have to go?"

"Not really. I don't want to go home, that's for sure. I'm so mad at my father," I said. He fiddled with the radio. Was I boring him?

"I know the perfect spot," he said and put the car into gear.

I took out my cell and left a message that I'd be out a little longer. I had a curfew, and there was no need to irritate my parents any further by pushing it.

The parking lot at Aliso Creek Beach was empty. We didn't get out of the car, but we could watch the waves from the front seat.

When I opened my mouth to speak, Theo kissed me and the thought went out of my head. Who knew Theo Roussos knew how to kiss like that?

Later, Theo's eyes were half-closed and he was breathing hard. Finally, he sat up. I noticed that sometime in the last half hour his shirt had mysteriously disappeared. Oh, right. It was on the floor where I'd thrown it after I'd yanked it off in a fit of lust. I felt like we'd gone from zero to sixty, like in all those car race movies.

"I think we need to slow down a bit," I said, although every nerve in my body was screaming in protest. My body wanted to return to that comfy seat and perhaps shed a few more clothes in the process.

"I would never hurt you, Chloe," Theo said.

But I knew he would, sooner or later.

"Not deliberately, I know," I said, "but I can't." I hesitated. I didn't want to voice what I was thinking.

"Why not?" he said.

"I don't know," I said. "This doesn't feel right." It did, it felt entirely too right.

"That's great, Chloe," Theo said. His voice was husky. "I have feelings for you."

What the hell did that mean? Just say it, my brain screamed, but he stayed silent. I stared at him. I was starting to panic.

"Who said anything about feelings?" I snapped, my pride tackling my common sense. "Theo, I don't know if I can trust you." My voice sounded harsh in the quiet night air.

"Why?" Theo said. "Why can't you trust me? We're friends."

"Yes, we are *friends*, Theo. And I can't afford to lose another friend."

"I'll take you home," Theo said after a long pause.

I looked at the clock and was surprised to see it was after one A.M. My mom was going to kill me.

When we reached my house, Theo turned off the engine and leaned back in his seat. I couldn't believe that he still wanted to talk after I'd lied and told him I wasn't interested in him. I'm probably gonna roast in the afterlife for that huge fib.

"Look, Chloe, I'm sorry about the way things worked out with Alex. But don't shut me out now."

"I don't know about all this," I said. "You're my *friend*, Theo." I was losing Bridget; what if I lost Theo, too?

"It won't happen again, not unless you want it to. But we need to talk about things, not fight." But when he reached for me, it was obvious that he didn't want to talk. And neither did I.

"We should stop." If we didn't stop soon, it would be too late. I was in over my head, and if I kissed Theo Roussos one more time, I couldn't predict what I'd do.

"Why?" Theo said. "Come back here," he said in a soft, sexy voice.

"No, I'm not ready for this," I said. "I've got to concentrate." How could I be anything other than friends with Theo when I *had to* beat Bridget? I had something to prove. If I got involved with Theo now, Bridget would win.

His lips tightened and he sat up. "All you can think of is Alex and this competition with Bridget. Forget about it. You don't really want Alex. If you did, you wouldn't be here with me."

"You should forget this," I said. "Forget about me."

"Maybe I will," he said, before getting out of my car and slamming the door.

I watched his back as he walked away. I waited, but he didn't return.

It had been an interesting birthday, but I wasn't sure it was one I wanted to repeat.

Chapter Sixteen

Thanksgiving break was almost here, which meant that I didn't have to face my problems at school for very long.

Nina was home from college. Dad was supposed to join us at Grandma's on Thanksgiving Day, but he called at the last minute to say he was running late. I seriously doubted he was going to show at all. Mom said we'd meet him there, and we drove inland along the winding Laguna Canyon Road to Grandma's place in Leisure World, a seniors-only complex in Laguna Hills. My grandma called it Geezer World.

Grandma's new boyfriend, Mr. Hernandez, would be there. We'd met him once before and he seemed like a kind man. We wondered what he saw in Grandma.

Thanksgiving at Grandma's meant Mom didn't have to cook and Grandma didn't have the chance to criticize Mom's cooking.

"Where's that ex-husband of yours? Off with his

new girlfriend?" Grandma asked as soon as we were in the door. She lived in a townhouse and her furniture was all white, which made me extremely nervous when eating. Grandma had a lot of expensive paintings, but none of them were my dad's.

"He's not my ex-husband, Mom," my mother said in a patient voice. "We're trying to work it out."

"It's only a matter of time," Grandma replied.

Nina and I exchanged glances. Another wonderful family holiday.

The doorbell rang and Mom jumped up to answer it. A few minutes later, she returned with my father.

"Devon," Grandma said coolly, "I'm pleased you could join us."

She didn't sound pleased. In fact, she sounded the opposite of pleased.

But Grandma's new boyfriend saved the day. He turned to my mom and said, "Rosemary tells me that you're a wonderful writer."

Everyone paused a beat to figure out who we knew named Rosemary who would be singing my mother's praises. My grandmother's name is Rosemary, but it still took a minute or two for our brains to process the information.

"She did?" my mom said, glancing at Grandma in amazement. A pleased smile broke out over my mother's face.

"I write children's books," I heard my mother say as Mr. Hernandez led her into the dining room. I caught Grandma trying to hide a smile and went over to give her a hug.

Grandma was a good cook, even though she'd be the first one to tell you so. After loads of turkey and stuffing and every side dish imaginable, it was time for dessert. Mom had brought a pumpkin pie, which she'd stayed up late to bake.

I prayed that for once Grandma would keep her thoughts to herself. She helped herself to a large piece, added a dollop of whipped cream, and took a cautious nibble.

It felt like everyone at the table was holding their breath.

"This is delicious," she said, and my mom beamed.

Thanksgiving dinner turned out okay after all. Grandma didn't make any nasty comments and Mom actually relaxed for a change. There was hope for my family yet.

My friendship with Bridget, however, was a lost cause. When school started again on Monday, I made one last attempt to salvage our friendship. No boy was worth it, I'd decided. I'd talk to Bridget and let her know that I wanted the weirdness between us to end.

I missed her, and I wanted things back the way they used to be.

I spotted Alex's car in the parking lot. He had gotten out of the driver's side and then gone around to open the door for Bridget. Now they were holding hands. They looked like the perfect couple, straight out of central casting. And that's when he saw me. He turned away and I knew it was over, but all I felt was a rush of relief.

I didn't get the chance to talk to her until school was over. I caught up with her at her locker after the dismissal bell.

"Bridget, can I talk to you for a minute?" I said.

She slammed her locker shut and then turned to face me. "It looks like you already are," she said. "So say what you have to say and quit wasting my time."

The words came out in a rush. "I want to be friends again. You can have Alex...."

My voice trailed off. I'd said exactly the wrong thing and I knew it even before his name crossed my lips.

"I know I can have him," she said. "And I already do." She started to walk away.

This wasn't going the way I'd expected. I lost my somewhat tenuous grip on my temper.

I blocked her path. "What's that supposed to mean?"

"Exactly what it sounds like," she replied. "The only reason you want to make up is because you know you've already lost."

"What are you talking about?"

"When's the last time he called you?" She sneered as she added, "You're outclassed and you know it."

"Bridget, don't be like that," I said, but she smirked at me and I lost my temper. "I've changed my mind." I threw the words at her before I stomped off.

There was no chance Bridget would forgive me now. I'd lost my best friend, and a niggling voice in my head told me that I'd lost her for a boy I didn't even respect. I needed to end it with Alex, end it officially. Maybe then Bridget would want to be friends again.

A stubborn part of me argued that friendship went two ways. Bridget wasn't making any attempt to heal the breach.

I heard a male voice calling my name when I walked into Gino's. My heart sped up when I realized it was Theo.

"Chloe, do you want to play a game?" Theo said, gesturing toward a pool table.

I hadn't talked to him since the night of my birthday party.

I said, "Have you seen Alex anywhere?"

"Hello, Theo," he said in a mocking voice. "I'm so glad to see you." He tried to be sarcastic, but under the sarcasm, he sounded hurt.

"Oh, sorry, Theo," I said. "That was rude. I'm sorry I'm so distracted."

But it was too late. I was talking to his back. I watched him stalk away. His shoulders were rigid. Great. Now I had another friend who wasn't speaking to me. I squelched the thought that Theo wasn't just a friend.

Chapter Seventeen

I needed something to take my mind off my problems. My sketchpad was gathering dust and I needed some new pencils, so I headed for Laguna Art Supplies and stocked up.

I cruised by the children's corner and checked it out. I remembered coming here with my dad when I was little. He'd plop me down there with my own little easel and pencils while he shopped for supplies. I'd drawn my first family portrait in that little corner.

Inspired by the memory, an idea for a drawing struck me and my hands itched for a pencil and some paper. I hadn't been excited about drawing in a long time. I was out of everything.

While I was browsing, something suddenly struck me. Kayley was going to be running for Frost Queen. Maybe I could help. I grabbed poster board and paints and added them to my cart.

When I got home I called Kayley.

"Can you come over now?" I said. "I have a surprise for you."

"I'll be there in ten minutes," she said.

Spending more time with her was the one bright spot in the whole disaster with Bridget.

When Kayley got there, my room was covered in poster board, markers, and jars of paint. I opened a paint lid and the familiar smell overwhelmed me. I screwed the lid back on tightly.

"It looks like an art store exploded in here," she said. "What's all this for?"

"We're going to make posters for your Frost Queen campaign," I said.

"Chloe, you're the best!" she said. "But I'm not running for Frost Queen." She was intrigued, though, I could tell.

"You are now," I said. "Hand me a brush." I felt a thrill to have the smooth wooden brush in my hand again.

"We need to think of a campaign slogan," Kayley said.

I didn't want the posters to look like everyone else's. I wanted something different.

I snapped my fingers. "A graphic novel," I said.

"What?"

"I'm going to make a series of posters, but they're going to be like a graphic novel," I said. "Each one will tell a story about you or something that happened at school."

"That's a great idea," Kayley said. She watched me

as I grabbed a pencil and drew a rough sketch on a piece of poster board. "I didn't know you were an artist. This one is great." She pointed to the drawing of me in my sketchbook.

"I stopped drawing for a while, when my parents split up," I admitted. "I was just so pissed off at my dad, and he's the one who taught me. It felt like I was betraying my mom every time I picked up my sketchpad. So I just stopped."

"How long has it been since you've done any new sketches?"

"Long enough that my sketchpad was covered in dust," I said. "And maybe part of it was a way to get back at my dad. But I think my parents are getting back together and I'm not sure who I should be mad at. Nobody, I guess."

Kayley was curious about my parents getting back together. "How do you feel about it? I mean, they go through the whole separation thing and now they're back together?"

"It's not going to be the same," I said.

"It never is," Kayley said. "But that doesn't mean it won't be okay, maybe even better." I knew she was right, but I didn't want to talk about my parents anymore.

I said, "That's depressing. Let's talk about something else besides me."

"Chloe, do you mind if I ask you something?" she said. "Why did you pick Alex over Theo?" She said

Alex's name like she was talking about a slug, which I guess is a pretty good description.

"I didn't know Theo was a choice," I said. "And besides, I thought Alex was somebody he wasn't."

"It's not your fault." She reached over and gave me a brief hug. "Alex likes to play games, and he's really good at making you feel like you're something special. But you caught on to him before anything major happened. Right?"

She was asking about sex, without putting it into words. I shook my head. "He'd been talking about it, but I told him not while he was still seeing both Bridget and me."

"You're better off without him," she said firmly.

"I know," I said. "But I think I blew it with Theo. I don't know why he likes me anyway. If he still does."

"What?" Kayley said. She stared at me. "I doubt Theo's given up on you. He's just hurt right now. And there are plenty of guys who might be interested. Rich, that guy from English class, is always staring at you."

"Rich Edmunds? Are you serious? He's never serious." From now on, my heart was going to be like Fort Knox, steely and impenetrable, but I still checked my cell phone all night, hoping for a call from Theo.

Chapter Eighteen

I didn't manage to track down Alex, so I sent him a "so long" e-mail. He didn't reply, but I hadn't really expected him to. It was kind of beating a dead horse, but the e-mail gave me closure, closure I needed, even if he and Bridget didn't.

Later that night, the upstairs phone rang. When I answered it, there was breathing on the other end. I slammed the phone down, cursing the fact that my parents were too cheap to get caller ID.

The phone rang again. "Who is this?" I said.

"It's me."

"Bridget?" I said.

"Don't hang up! Please," she said.

I sighed. "What do you want?"

"I gave Alex an ultimatum," she said. "No more flirting with other girls."

"Bridget, are you crying?"

"No," she said. "Of course not."

There was silence between us.

"I *was* crying," she said. "And I wanted to talk to my best friend about it, but I don't have a best friend anymore."

"I miss you, you know," I said softly.

For a minute, I didn't think she was going to answer. "I miss you, too," she said, "I can't —"

She hung up.

I grabbed the phone to call her back. As I picked it up, it rang again.

"Hello," I said eagerly. Maybe we still had a chance to salvage something of our friendship.

But it wasn't Bridget.

"What's up? You sounded kinda weird." It was Kayley.

"Sorry. Someone called a minute ago and — never mind."

"Was it Bridget?"

How did she know?

"It was her on the phone before," I admitted. "She hung up, though."

"Bridget doesn't like to lose," Kayley observed.

"Neither do I," I said. "That's one of the reasons we're friends."

"*Were* friends," Kayley pointed out, not unkindly. "You can't think you two can still be friends after all this?"

I hesitated. "We've been friends a long time. And I

did go out with Alex, even after I knew Bridget liked him. I'm partly responsible."

"But you didn't mean to hurt her," Kayley said. "Look, if I tell you something, will you promise not to get more upset than you already are?"

"I won't get upset," I lied, convincingly, I guess, because Kayley continued.

"I think Bridget was willing to go further than you were to keep Alex," she said. "And I think she already has."

At first, I didn't get what she was trying to say.

There was a tight feeling in my chest and I felt like crying. Alex and Bridget were having sex? It shouldn't hurt, since I'd figured out he was a user, but it did.

I didn't ask Kayley how she knew. By now, I knew that she wouldn't have said anything unless the information came from a reliable source.

"Tell me everything," I said.

"Vinnie told me," she admitted. "Theo told him that he accidentally walked in on Alex and Bridget."

"When?" I asked, between clenched teeth.

"After some party, I guess," Kayley said. "But," she added hurriedly, "Vinnie didn't say anything until a couple of days ago."

"Alex is a complete skank," I said. "He's sleeping with Bridget, but it sounds like he's still flirting with other girls."

"What are you going to do?"

"Nothing," I said. What could I do? Bridget and I were worlds apart in attitude, outlook, and, now it seemed, experience. It made me realize that Bridget and I would never be friends again. If we ever were.

"Vinnie was worried you'd be mad at him for not saying anything."

I was mad, but I knew who was really to blame. "Of course not," I said. "But Alex Harris is another story."

"Wow, you've had a really crappy day," Kayley said. "I was going to ask you something, but maybe now's not the time."

"Ask away," I said airily. I wasn't going to let Bridget ruin my life.

"Would you consider going to the dance with Theo?" she said. "I'm going with Vinnie and we thought it would be fun if we doubled."

Our high school always had a semiformal in December, before school let out for the winter break.

"Did he ask you to ask me?" I said.

"No, but it's a great idea," Kayley replied.

I thought about it for a minute. *Why* hadn't he asked me? It was illogical, I know, since I had been completely obsessed with Alex only a few weeks ago, but I was discovering that I liked the blond surfer-boy look after all. And I liked Theo. Obviously, since I'd spent the night of my birthday making out with him.

"I thought Theo had given up on me," I said. "I've

been kind of self-absorbed lately. And Lia still seems interested."

"I told you," Kayley said. "She's not his type."

I felt a happy little glow at the news.

"Besides, I can't say yes yet anyway," I said.

"Why not?"

"I don't have anything to wear."

Kayley laughed and, before she hung up, promised to take me shopping.

I'd already put my pajamas on when the phone rang again.

"Hello?" I said.

There was silence, then "Chloe?"

"Theo, is that you?" Suddenly, I was wide-awake.

"I know I'm calling kind of late."

"No, it's okay," I said in a rush.

There was a pause and then he blurted out, "Would you go to the dance with me? We'll double with Vinnie and Kayley."

"Yes," I said. "I'd love to. Theo . . ." I wanted to tell him how wrong I'd been, how stupid, but I lost my nerve.

"Yeah?"

"Never mind. I'll see you at school."

I placed the phone into its cradle and smiled as I turned out the light.

* * *

Most girls would be obsessed with finding the perfect dress for the dance, but I just wanted to find something I could wear without feeling like a complete phony.

I still hadn't found it when Nina and Kayley dragged me dress shopping.

"Consider it an early Christmas present," Nina said.

I looked at her suspiciously. "You already spent too much on me for my birthday present, remember?" I said, touching the silver earrings in the shape of pool cues. I never took them off.

"And you, too," I said to Kayley. I smoothed down the soft green sweater Kayley had given me for my birthday.

"We know you're saving for a new stereo for your car. Dad gave me the money for your dress. Our gift is the benefit of our combined style and shopping experience."

I bristled a little at the mention of my father. I wasn't angry with him anymore, but I wasn't sure I was ready to take his money again. Then I thought, *What the heck?* I did need a new dress. I'd never admit it, but I wanted to make an impression at the dance.

"Okay, let's go. You have two hours," I said. Both Kayley and Nina were marathon shoppers.

There wasn't an actual mall in Laguna Beach, so we drove up the freeway to South Coast Plaza. It's hard to believe, but I found the perfect dress in the first store we went into.

Kayley had bought her dress the day Vinnie asked her to go to the dance. She still wanted to go to other stores, but I stubbornly refused to move until I'd tried it on.

"Look, it's perfect. It's the same color as the sweater you gave me." I held the dress up next to the sweater I wore.

"It's pretty plain, but you can't tell anything on the hanger," Nina said, shepherding me toward the dressing room. "And don't forget, you still need some shoes. And I mean real shoes with heels, not flats."

I came out of the dressing room, hoping that this would be it. The dress. Instead, the fashion queens gave it a thumbs-down.

"It's the same color as the felt on a pool table," Nina said, reading my mind. "No way."

"But it's comfortable," I said.

"It's the color of pond scum," Kayley added. "Don't try to fool us by picking out the first decent dress you see. We want divine, not decent. You're going to knock Theo Roussos's socks right off him."

"And maybe a few other articles of clothing," Nina said, snickering.

I said, "I'm not ready to start getting serious with anyone right now. I need to concentrate on the tournament." My protestations sounded weak even to me.

"I don't know," Kayley said teasingly, "I caught a definite vibe between you and Theo."

"You're better off with Theo," Nina said bluntly. "Alex is a tool. An attractive tool, but a tool, nevertheless."

"Bridget better watch out," Kayley said thoughtfully.

Nina and I both looked at her. "What do you mean?"

"He's a user," she replied. "He used Chloe." I winced at the bare pronouncement of my own stupidity.

"And he'll use Bridget, too. Until he gets what he wants and then he'll drop her. If you ask me, Bridget did you a favor."

Alex had fooled me into thinking he was someone else, but it was hard to take any comfort in that fact.

"I guess she did," I said. "But I don't know why our friendship had to end over it."

Kayley stared at me in exasperation. "You still haven't given up?"

"No, I've given up," I said. "Hey, there's the carousel," I said, firmly changing the subject. I didn't want to think about Alex anymore. He was in the past. I had no romantic interest in him any longer, but I was still determined to win the tournament, if only to rub my former best friend's face in it.

"Let's go for a ride."

Nina and Kayley looked doubtful. "We still haven't found you a dress," Nina said.

"My feet are killing me," I said. "I need a break. Besides, it'll be fun. Remember, Nina, when Dad and Mom used to take us here when we were little?"

I took their hands and dragged them over. I bought three tickets from the attendant.

"I remember when you barfed on my new Mary Jane's," Nina said, turning to Kayley to explain. "They were my favorite shoes, red leather with shiny buckles."

"That's gross," Kayley exclaimed.

"Chloe rode on that pony right there." Nina pointed to a pink-and-white horse. I ran over to it and climbed on.

Nina and Kayley grabbed the horses next to me and then Nina continued the story. "But then Chloe wouldn't get off. She rode on that horse about fifty times until Dad finally carried her off. And then she threw up all over me."

The ride started and as we whirled around, I saw it in a store window, directly across from the carousel. It was the perfect dress, a deep green dream, which shone through the shop window.

I was off in a shot when the ride ended.

I heard Nina say, "Chloe, wait up," but I didn't slow my pace. My heart raced. I didn't want anybody else to get to the dress before I did.

Kayley and Nina caught up to me. "It'll be perfect," Nina pronounced.

And it was. An hour later, my stomach was growling, my dad's credit card was smoking, and my feet were killing me, but I had a dress to wear to the dance.

I hadn't thought about Alex and Bridget in at least an hour. Whenever I thought of them, I pictured them comparing notes about how gullible I was. And I had finally realized that Bridget and I would never be the same. Our friendship wasn't strong enough to put back together again.

"Let's stop at the food court. I'm starving," I said.

And that was where I ran into Bridget.

At the food court, we split up to order from our favorite places. I was in line at the burger stand when Bridget walked up to me.

"Hey, Chloe. What are you doing here?" she said.

"Shopping for a dress for the dance," I said. What did she want?

She said, "I'm going with Alex, of course."

"Has he asked you yet?" I said, dying to know the answer.

"Not yet, but it's only a matter of time," she said. Had Bridget been this cocky when we were best friends?

I didn't say anything. Obviously, Bridget had more to say, but for some reason, she wasn't getting straight to the point.

"What's up, Bridget?" I said directly.

"Did you see they announced the finalists for the tournament?" she said. "It was posted after school yesterday."

I'd been too busy buying a dress. I couldn't believe I forgot to check. I shook my head, but I could tell by the smug way she looked at me that Alex made it in.

"Did I get in?" I asked.

"You'll have to check on Monday," she said.

"Monday?" I said, and then tried not to let my disappointment show. For a moment, the old Bridget appeared.

"You made it," she said. But then she disappeared as quickly as she had appeared, when she added, "I'll give you a little advice. Drop out of the tournament."

Drop out? I actually made it in! There wasn't a chance in hell I was going to drop out now.

"Look, Bridget, I know you're trying, but—"

"If you win the tournament, we're not friends anymore," she said.

"Haven't you noticed? We haven't been friends for a long time," I said.

Nina and Kayley walked up to us, carrying their trays.

Bridget walked off, but said over her shoulder, "Think about what I said, okay? I always get what I want. And I want Alex to win that tournament." It sounded like a threat.

When lunch was over, we went back to shopping. Evidently, I still needed an arsenal of makeup and beauty products, along with a pair of lethal-looking heels.

By the end of the day, I was exhausted, but I still tried on the dress when I got home. I examined myself in the mirror.

It was a dress sure to make Theo's eyes pop right out of his head. I slipped off the dress and hung it in my closet, careful not to crush the fabric. I put on some comfy sweats and a camisole and spent the rest of the night dreaming about what it would be like to actually go out on a date with Theo, a guy I'd known forever. A guy I was just starting to see differently.

Chapter Nineteen

My favorite place to go for ice cream was the Shake Shack, which was a little place right on the beach. It was open all year and I was starving, so Kayley and I headed there for an afternoon pick-me-up. It was cold and overcast, but the Shake Shack had the best date shakes.

We walked to the window and placed our order.

"I can't believe it," I said. "They painted the shack a different color."

The Shake Shack had been bright yellow since I was a kid.

Kayley said, "Things change, Chloe."

"I don't like change," I said stubbornly.

"No offense," Kayley said, "but maybe that's part of your problem."

"What do you mean?"

"The thing with Bridget," she said, hesitating before she finally continued. "You guys haven't really been friends for a long time. It was habit, at least on Bridget's part."

"Maybe," I said. "But we were friends once. Real friends."

"I know," she said. "I know you were."

When our shakes came, we walked down to the water and watched the surfers. I shivered at the thought of being in the water in December.

I couldn't finish my shake. My stomach rejected the creamy mixture, so I threw it in the trash and it landed with a dull thud.

"Are you okay?" Kayley said. "You always finish your food."

It was the day of the dance, but I hadn't heard from Theo. I wondered if he regretted ever getting involved with me, especially since my little love triangle with Alex seemed to be hot gossip, now that it was finally over.

I stared at the waves, churning and crashing against the sand. "I haven't talked to Theo since he asked me to the dance. I'm not even sure he's going to show."

"He'll show," Kayley said. "If he doesn't, I'll personally hunt him down and hurt him. We should go. We need to start getting ready for the dance."

I looked at my watch. Did I really need two hours to take a shower and put on a dress? Amazingly, I did.

We went to my house to get ready. If Theo didn't show, I was going to the dance anyway. Even if I had to ride to the dance with Kayley and Vinnie in the limo. I tried not to think about how pathetic that would be.

Nina supervised while Kayley and I did our hair and put on our makeup. I tried to smile and laugh and pretend nothing was wrong, but I was worried about Theo.

Why had I waited until the big dance to talk to him? What if he wouldn't talk to me? It was too much pressure.

Kayley looked beautiful in a long blue dress. I didn't want to ruin Kayley's big night, but I was a bundle of nerves. I peeked out the window. A white limo pulled up to our house. The doorbell rang a minute later. I dropped the curtain.

"Chloe, the boys are here," Mom said.

Kayley and I went downstairs and Nina trailed after us like an anxious mother hen.

I had been worried that Theo wouldn't show, but Mom had been right; it was boys in the plural. Theo stood next to Vinnie, wearing a black tux.

"You both look gorgeous. Don't leave until I get my camera," Mom said. "I want a few photos of you and Kayley and the boys."

Nina rolled her eyes. "Go on, she'll never let you out of the house unless you pose for the photo album," she said. "Besides, you look fantastic."

I looked over at Theo. He hadn't said a word.

"Hi," I said.

"Hi," he said. "I like your dress. It's the same color as your eyes."

Why had it taken me so long to really see Theo? Alex hadn't known the color of my eyes. He hadn't known anything about me. But Theo did. I impulsively kissed his cheek

We both froze, staring into each other's eyes. I smelled a warm clean Theo smell, like sunlight and sand. I was beginning to figure out it was one of my favorite smells. I was the one who finally looked away.

My parents wrapped their arms around each other and beamed at us.

What on earth was going on? My life had turned into a complete joke. My parents were acting like Romeo and Juliet, but I was trying to figure out what was going on.

And Theo seemed to have lost all conversational skills. I had a hard time believing that Kayley was right. Theo wasn't acting like someone with a huge crush. He actually looked a little bored.

I shrugged. I was going to the dance, even if I had a reluctant date. Theo's loss, right? I couldn't brush away the feeling that it was my loss, too. And if we had a prayer of staying friends, I needed to explain everything to him.

The limo driver hopped out and opened the car door. At least I was being driven in style.

"Uh, are we going straight to the dance?" I said. I realized I hadn't had anything to eat for hours.

"Theo and I planned on having dinner at Gino's first," Vinnie replied.

"That's Chloe's favorite!" Kayley said happily. "And I love their vegetable pasta."

I knew it was a little shallow to think about food at a time like this, but I was starving. In Nina's mind, the shake should have tided me over until dinner. She had finished with my makeup about five minutes before the limo got here, with stern instructions not to ruin my lipstick by eating.

Theo was in the far corner of the limo, which was as far away from me as he possibly could get and still be in the limo. Kayley was practically sitting in Vinnie's lap and their faces glowed with the pleasure of being together. Kayley and Vinnie must have twisted his arm hard to get him to go to the dance with me. I didn't blame him for being mad.

Kayley and Vinnie were absorbed in each other and wouldn't have noticed anything less than an earthquake, let alone the fact that my date seemed to be not into me at all. Theo sat back in his seat, a little smile on his lips.

The door opened and Vinnie and Kayley slid out. I continued to stare into space. I finally heard the sound of a throat being cleared.

"Uh, Chloe?" I looked up.

"Are you ready to eat?" Theo asked. My mouth dropped open as he took my hand.

"I'm starving," I said. I tugged on his hand, stopping him from following Kayley and Vinnie into the restaurant.

"Theo, why did you ask me to the dance?"

"I guessed that my subtle hints weren't working," he said.

"H-hints? About what?" I said.

"That I'm crazy about you, even if you are the most competitive person I know," he said. He didn't let go of my hand as we entered the restaurant.

I stopped. "I'm an idiot," I said.

Theo wanted to be with me. He was crazy about me, in fact. I took that in while we were shown to our table.

We were seated in one of Gino's cozy red leather booths. It was the booth in the corner of the restaurant, intimate and cozy. Vinnie and Kayley were already snuggling away.

Gino came and took our order. My heart jolted when Theo ordered my favorite pizza, "Please, no garlic."

When the food came, I dished out slices of pizza onto plates and handed them around the table. We were quiet as we snarfed.

"I think we should have ordered two pizzas," Theo said, finally pushing his empty plate away and leaning back.

"It's my favorite," I said.

Theo smiled. "It's my favorite, too." He called the server over to the table. "It looks like we'll need desserts. Four chocolate heavens, please."

"I've never tried that before. What is it?" I was curious. "I thought I'd eaten everything on Gino's menu," I said.

"It's not on the menu, but Gino will make it if you ask. I hope you like chocolate," he said.

"Oh, I do."

Kayley giggled. "Chloe is a chocolate fiend."

My mouth watered as the server returned with four heaping bowls of chocolate heaven.

It was a wonderful concoction of rich gooey chocolate brownies, white chocolate shavings, and raspberry sauce. Kayley took deliberate bites, savoring the taste, before pushing the bowl over to Vinnie to finish.

Theo pretended to be in awe of how much I could eat as I scooped the last bit of raspberry sauce from my bowl.

"That was the most delicious thing I've ever tasted," I commented.

"I've never seen anybody finish one of those before," Theo said.

"Well, get used to it," I said, then blushed at my own presumption. "I mean . . ."

"I promise we'll order one on our next date," he said teasingly. "We can even play pool, if you want."

"Prepare to lose," Kayley said.

"Oh, don't count on it," Vinnie said. "Theo's a great pool player. Better than Alex any day."

We all grew silent at the mention of his name. I looked at Theo nervously, but he met my eyes with a steady gaze.

"Theo, why didn't you enter the pool tournament?" It didn't really matter.

"Why would I do something like that?" Theo said. "I like pool, but I don't feel the need to compete. Volleyball does it for me. Pool's for fun."

"But I love to compete. Won't it bother you if I win when we play pool?"

He thought about it for a minute. "Chloe, I can take it if you beat me at pool." Then he added softly, "I don't care about any game as much as I care about you."

That's when I kissed him. Right in front of Kayley and Vinnie, who tactfully pretended not to stare.

I did find the right guy after all.

After dinner, we headed to the dance. I almost didn't recognize the school gym. Shiny red and silver ribbons dangled from the ceiling and there were balloons and tinsel everywhere. Strands of white lights twinkled from every available surface and there were so many rose petals on the ground that it looked like a flower girl had run amuck.

"It looks like Santa exploded in here," I said to Theo.

"I like it," he said, tucking my hand into his.

I smiled up at him. "I like it, too."

Kayley and Vinnie wandered off in search of a discreetly darkened corner. Theo grabbed my hand and led me to the dance floor. He pulled me into his arms and I rested my head on his shoulder. It felt right to be in his arms.

A few songs later, he said, "I'll be right back. Do you want some punch?"

I stood at the edge of the dance floor and watched my parents. They were slow dancing, oblivious to the idea that chaperones should be watching the kids instead of each other. It was a huge relief to know they wouldn't be paying too much attention to Theo and me.

I saw Bridget and Alex arrive and walk onto the dance floor. Bridget wore a long white gown and had white roses in her hair. Diamonds sparkled in her ears. She and Alex looked like something torn from the pages of a teen magazine, if you ignored the grim expressions on their faces.

She caught Alex staring at some freshman's cleavage and gave him a quick slap on the wrist. Despite her sparkles, there was an unhappy look in her eyes. I wanted to go over to her, but knew that it was too soon.

I turned away and saw Theo walking toward me. There was a cardboard snowflake dangling over his head. It seemed to be telling me something.

He came back without the punch, but wearing a huge smile. I gave him an inquiring look. Then the DJ put a different song on. It was "Standing on the Edge of Love."

"I thought you might like this song," Theo said.

"From *The Color of Money* soundtrack," I finished his sentence. "But how did you convince the DJ to play it?"

"I have my ways," Theo said. He took me in his arms and we swayed to the music, barely moving. My nerve endings hummed at the feel of his body next to mine.

When the song ended, Ms. Ryan, the principal, got up on the stage.

"I'd like to introduce the court at this time. Please join me on the stage," she said. "We'll be holding the coronation of this year's Frost Queen momentarily."

Kayley, Bridget, Lia, and four senior girls I didn't know went up on the stage. There was a row of chairs and Lia and Bridget sat together. Kayley sat on the opposite side, next to one of the seniors.

Ms. Ryan said, "I would like to announce the Frost Court — Lia Cruz, Kayley Nichols, Amy Nguyen, Traci Shannon, Bridget Stewart, and Alyssa Zalvadar."

Theo gave a loud whistle and Vinnie beamed and let out a huge yell. Lia, Bridget, and Amy (the beautiful girl sitting next to Kayley) all rated howls and piercing whistles.

I was crossing my fingers that Kayley had won. I was glad her campaign had brought me back to drawing and inspired me to try something new.

I turned my attention back to the principal and caught the end of her speech. "I'd like to announce Laguna Beach High School's Frost Queen . . ."

During the suspenseful pause, I leaned forward in my seat and glanced at Bridget. She was sitting in her chair onstage, smiling calmly, her hands placed in her lap, but they were clenched tightly into fists.

Ms. Ryan fumbled with the envelope and then said into the microphone. "May I present Amy Nguyen, this year's Frost Queen."

The gym rang with loud applause as Amy went to the podium to receive her crown and bouquet. I clapped as loudly as anybody. I was disappointed that Kayley wasn't Queen of the Frost Ball, but I didn't want Bridget to win either.

Afterward, I went up to Amy, who was glowing in

her shiny crown. She carried a dozen long-stemmed roses. "Congratulations," I said.

"Thanks," she said. "I really liked the campaign posters you did for Kayley. Are you going to art school next year?"

"I'm a junior, but I think I am going to art school." Which was something I just realized.

She said, "Good luck in art school."

"Thanks, and congratulations again." I stepped back as she was surrounded by well-wishers.

I noticed that Bridget wasn't among the group wishing Amy well, but then reminded myself that Bridget wasn't my problem anymore.

Theo came up behind me and wrapped his arms around my waist. "Want to dance?"

We danced until the gym was nearly empty, but I still didn't want to go home. He whispered in my ear and I nodded. We headed over to Kayley and Vinnie, who were swaying to the music, dreamy looks on their faces.

"We're going to take off," I said. "We'll send the limo back for you guys."

Chapter Twenty

$\mathcal{I}$t was almost Christmas, one of Dad's favorite holidays. Mine, too. This year, I hadn't even thought about the holiday much, despite the sounds of Christmas music everywhere. I'd probably been blocking it out. Even seeing a sprig of holly made me wince.

He was spending the holidays with us, but that didn't change the fact that he didn't live with us. Mom kept pretending that nothing had changed, but I knew better. I was still getting used to the idea that Christmas, and our family, would never be the same again.

Dad and I were in charge of the festivities every year. Nina and Mom helped, of course, but right before Christmas, Dad and I would pick out the biggest tree we could find.

This year, preparing for Christmas Eve dinner was an unusually tense event at our house. I watched my mom become a whirlwind of baking, wrapping, and shopping. She was trying too hard. I suggested that Gino cater the McBride Christmas Eve dinner this year, but Mom wouldn't hear of it. She was pulling out all the stops.

The great Devon McBride would be putting in an appearance and my mother thought this holiday had to be perfect.

"Ten to one he doesn't show," I muttered to Nina as I pulled the nineteenth tray of sugar cookies out of the oven.

She shot me a pained look. That's when I realized that my mom was within earshot. She winced, but didn't say anything to me. I felt horrible. I didn't want to take out my bad mood on my mom. It wasn't her fault. Dad was the one I wanted to skewer with candy canes. And he, as usual, was nowhere in sight.

I wandered into the living room. A huge pine tree towered there, but we hadn't decorated it yet. Devon McBride couldn't be bothered to make a personal appearance to pick out a tree. Instead, it was delivered early the week before. Mom insisted that I wait for Dad to decorate it. Someone, probably Mom, had hauled the boxes of decorations out of the attic.

I decided to hang the lights. It was harder to do alone, but I didn't want to ask for help. Mom would probably tell me to wait for Dad. I figured I'd been waiting long enough. It was Christmas Eve.

After I finally managed to get the lights wound around the tree, I flipped the switch and stood in the darkened living room and watched the twinkling lights. I turned on some holiday music and unpacked the ornaments. I held up a hand-painted fairy ornament. My father had made it for me when I was twelve.

I remembered that even then, I had no interest in fairies. I'd wanted solids and stripes for ornaments, but my dad had suddenly acted like my love of pool was a crime. He tried to steer me toward pinks and purples, but I wanted the primary colors.

"Chloe, what are you doing? I thought you were going to wait for your father." I froze at the sound of my mom's voice.

I exaggeratedly looked at my watch. "Mom, if we wait much longer, Christmas will be over."

"Why do you have to be like this? He's a little late, that's all. Give him a break," she said, her voice rising.

"He has had every break possible. Aren't you sick of making excuses for him?" I couldn't stop the cruel words as they spewed from my mouth.

My mom's face turned white. She stood there, not saying a word, while tears rolled down her cheeks. She whispered, "It's not his fault."

I took an ornament and threw it. It shattered against the wall.

"Chloe, your father gave you that!" My mother's voice was shocked and I knew I'd gone too far. I wanted to apologize to her, but the words clogged in my throat.

Instead, I grabbed my jacket and ran out of the house.

Hot tears exploded. I was crying because I'd hurt my mom, but also because my dad had hurt me. As much as I wanted to deny it, I'd hoped to see him on Christmas Eve. I didn't want to stick around waiting for my father to disappoint me again.

I didn't know where to go, but my feet took me to the door of Gino's. It was closed, of course.

But I stood there anyway and looked into the window, not knowing where else to go. Finally, I turned away. I needed to call home and let everyone know I was okay. I fished for my cell phone in my jacket pocket.

I called Nina on her cell. She answered on the first ring.

"Chloe, where are you? Dad's here and we're holding dinner." Nina's voice was tense.

"Eat without me. I don't want to see him. Tell Mom I'll be back later. I've got to go." I hung up before Nina could argue with me.

Downtown Laguna was mostly deserted. There were only a few last-minute shoppers bustling around looking for an open store. I spotted the statue of the Greeter, the one in front of the Greeter's Corner Restaurant.

Ever since we were little, Bridget and I would jump up and try to slap his hand, which was raised in a permanent wave. The Greeter's real name was Eilar Larsen and there were two statues of him in Laguna Beach. I looked around, but no one was watching, so I gave the statue a high five as I walked by.

I knew I'd have the beach to myself this time of year. I crossed the highway and headed for the sand.

I passed by the playground and, on impulse, sat in one of the swings. The sky was gray, exactly matching my mood. I dangled my legs in the sand and watched the waves. Their reliable motion soothed me.

"I thought I'd find you here," Theo's voice interrupted my thoughts.

"Hi," I said. "Why were you looking for me?" The words had sounded harsh and I winced. "I'm sorry."

"Your dad called me."

"Oh," I said.

"I told him I'd look for you. He was worried about you," Theo explained gently.

"I got into a fight with my mom," I said.

Theo nodded. "I figured." He hesitated. "Divorce is hard on everybody," he said. "But it does get better. If you ever need someone to talk to..." his voice trailed off.

"I almost wish it were divorce," I said.

Theo looked confused. "I thought..."

"They're getting back together, can you believe it? After all that they put us through?"

"People change," Theo said.

"I don't," I said.

"Maybe you should," he said. "Change isn't all bad."

I started to ask him how he knew anything about it, but stopped before I could blurt out the question. Of course, Theo knew. His family had been through a divorce about six months ago. We'd known each other forever and I hadn't, not once, even told him I was sorry about it.

"Theo, I was really sorry to hear about your parents," I said. "I know it's a little late. I guess I didn't know what to say."

"It's okay," he said. "No one ever does."

To avoid his gaze, I looked at the moon. There was a pink glow to it. I hummed this old Nick Drake song that my dad used to sing.

"What's that song?" Theo said.

"'Pink Moon.' It's —"

"A Nick Drake song. I like that song," he said.

"Not many people have heard of it," I said.

"Not many," he said, "but we have." And that's when he kissed me, a slow, tender kiss.

We broke apart and then I stared at the water for a moment.

Finally, Theo said, "Chloe, can I ask you something?"

"Of course," I said.

"Forget it," Theo said abruptly.

"No, go ahead."

He paused, then blurted out. "Are you playing in the tournament to get back at Bridget? Or to impress Alex?"

"No, of course not," I said. "I want to win that tournament for me."

He looked at his hands. "Are you sure?"

"Yes, I'm sure," I said. "Do you have something you want to ask me, Theo?"

"No. Never mind. Let's get out of here. I'll walk you home."

What had Theo been about to say?

We hiked up the hill to my house and stopped in front of my driveway. I fished for my key.

"I'll see you around. Good night, Chloe." He kissed me and then strode away. As I watched him walk away, I wondered what it would be like to kiss him again. To kiss him and not stop this time.

I saw the curtain move in the family room. Nina was probably waiting up for me.

"Did you have a good time?" my dad said as he stepped from the shadows.

"Yes, did you?" I sounded snotty, but I didn't care. He stared at me.

"I know I've let you down lately, but I'm still your father," he said finally.

I stared at him. "Devon, fatherhood is about more

than biology," I said. "Did you think about us even once when you decided to leave?"

"Everything's not as black and white as you think it is," he said.

"Well, it should be," I said. "I'm going to bed."

"Chloe, your mother asked me to leave."

"Dad?" The dad slipped out. I couldn't help it. He looked so unhappy. I thought that would make me happy, my dad being miserable, but it didn't.

"I love your mother, Chloe. And I love you girls. And I always will," he said. "And now I'm going to bed. Merry Christmas." He walked slowly up the stairs and I realized he was getting older.

"Good night, Dad. And Merry Christmas," I called out softly, but he was already gone.

I sat in the living room and watched the Christmas lights twinkling. My mind tried to process everything my father had said. It was a long time before I went to sleep that night.

Chapter Twenty-One

We always unwrapped presents first thing Christmas morning. I was in a panic. I hadn't bought my father anything, and after our conversation last night, I was reconsidering my anti–Devon McBride stance. I felt pretty cruddy about the way I had treated him. I had been wrong about him.

A divorce was hard on any family, but I had blamed everything on my dad. And now I owed him an apology or twelve.

I went down to the kitchen. I'd make a pot of coffee and then walk downtown. Maybe I'd get lucky and find someplace open on Christmas Day. I needed a gift for my dad and it couldn't be something that smacked of last-minute guilt.

My mom was already downstairs. She'd made coffee and had the turkey in the oven. She was still in her pajamas.

"I invited Theo over," she said. "I hope that's okay. He's alone today. His mom had to fly out of town on business."

"Sure," I said. "But Theo's mom has to work on *Christmas*? That sucks." Theo never talked about his mom's job very much.

"About last night—" Mom said.

"Why didn't you tell me that you asked Dad to leave?" I burst out. "He took the blame, and it was your fault the whole time."

"Chloe, the separation wasn't anybody's fault. I asked your father to leave, it's true, but it wasn't anybody's fault." She poured a cup of coffee and sat at the counter.

"Didn't you love him anymore?" I said.

"Of course I did," she said. "It's not always about love or lack of love. I felt lost."

"What do you mean?" I sat next to her.

"Did you know that we were starving artists when your father and I first met?" she said.

"Paris, right?" I said softly. "All you and Dad ever talked about was how romantic it was."

"When you were little, we decided, I decided, that I'd put my career on hold until his was established. But pretty soon, I didn't know what I wanted. I kept giving up the things I loved, until I didn't know who I was anymore," she said. "I think I was scared to compete with him."

I was mad at her, but I was also mad at myself. She had tried to tell me, but I hadn't listened. Besides, I was tired of being angry with my parents.

"I'm sorry I didn't tell you the truth, but your dad and I were trying to protect you. And maybe I wanted you on my side. I'm ashamed of myself."

I went over and gave my mom a long hug. I said softly, "It's okay, Mom. But I was so mad at Dad that I didn't get him anything for Christmas. I need to figure something out."

The phone rang. It was Theo making sure it still was okay to come over.

"Sure," I said. "We can go to the beach later." Then I remembered what happened yesterday when we went to the beach. I hoped Theo didn't think I was suggesting another make-out session. Or maybe I did.

After I hung up, I stared at a family photo I'd taken and hung on the refrigerator. What was I going to do for a present for Dad?

I'd make him a collage of our family pictures. I looked at my watch. I had enough time.

I went to the computer. Mom had tons of family photos scanned into its hard drive. I found a few favorites, clicked PRINT, and took them up to my room, along with some scissors and glue. Nina popped her head into my room a few minutes later.

"What are you doing?" she said.

"I didn't get anything for Dad," I explained.

"He's Dad again?" she said, confused.

"Did you get him anything?" I said.

"Yep. Some Reactions memorabilia I found at this collectible store by the college," she said. "Want me to add your name to it?"

The Reactions was my dad's favorite band. "No, I want to make him something, to make up for my snotty ass attitude," I said. As I worked, I filled her in on what Mom had told me.

"Unbelievable," Nina said. She looked thoughtful. "I kind of wondered if something else was going on. Mom was acting weird, but I was so pissed at Dad."

"Yeah, me, too," I said. We sat silently for a few minutes.

"Let me help," she said, grabbing a pair of scissors. We finished the collage about five minutes before Dad called us down to breakfast.

We opened our presents after breakfast. Nina jumped up and down over the gift certificates to this funky little boutique in Laguna that she loved. Mom was all excited about the new artist-chick top, and my dad was thrilled over the collage Nina helped me make for him.

"I love it," he said. "Chloe, maybe you should think about photography as a career. After you go to art school . . ." he trailed off when he saw my face. My dad was trying to turn me into an artist. I wasn't sure *what* I was yet, but I didn't think one or two decent photos made me a photographer.

In the center was a copy of the family photo he kept in his studio, and I'd cut out pictures of Mom and Nina and me and glued them in a random pattern around the frame. I felt a little guilty about getting such an enthusiastic reaction to a last-minute gift, but I was glad he liked it.

Theo showed up at about noon. He wore a red sweater and looked like my perfect Christmas present.

I led him into the house, hoping that nobody in my family would say or do anything embarrassing. And right on cue I remembered that my grandma would be there eventually. While we waited, Theo and I set the table while Mom and Dad snuggled in the kitchen.

Grandma and Mr. Hernandez showed up about an hour later. She was never on time for anything. She drove her big white Caddy about two miles an hour.

Grandma was already checking out Theo's butt in a very obvious way.

"Mom, she's your mother," I whispered urgently. "Tell her to stop."

"Stop what? She hasn't done anything yet," my mom said. But there was a smile on her face.

I loved Grandma, but man, she was a handful. I was betting the turkey wouldn't even be on the table before she was asking about my nonexistent sex life. In front of Theo, a guy I'd kissed and, I hoped, would kiss many times again.

I introduced her to Theo, holding my breath that she wouldn't say anything too outrageous. They'd met before, but I wasn't sure Grandma would remember. I think Theo was about twelve the last time she'd seen him and he'd filled out considerably since then.

"I like him," she pronounced, after looking Theo up and down for several minutes. I'd swear Grandma was checking out more than Theo's character, if the way her eyes lingered below his waist was any indication.

"Thank you, Mrs. Bishop," Theo replied politely.

"Call me Rosemary. Everyone does," she said. She turned to me and said in a fake stage whisper that they could probably hear all the way in the kitchen, "I like him. This one looks like he has staying power." Then she waggled her eyebrows, in case we were completely clueless. Somehow, my grandmother's seal of approval wasn't that reassuring.

Thankfully, Mom called us in to dinner. It smelled heavenly. Theo sat next to my grandmother and I prayed she wouldn't put her hand on his knee (or anywhere else).

Then Dad made us go around the table and say

something about what the favorite part of our year had been. He did this every Christmas. I smiled as I looked around the table. I thought that maybe our family stood a chance to be happy again.

"Mom, this looks delicious. And normal. Not an ounce of caviar to be found," I said. Everyone laughed.

Grandma picked up her plate and sniffed it suspiciously, but then must have decided it was edible, because she dug in. My mom frowned when she watched her mother, but then my dad distracted her with a compliment about the mashed potatoes. Overall, my grandma behaved herself and refrained from any snide remarks about my mom's cooking and/or career choices.

We ate tons and then we all went for a walk on the beach. Even my grandma and Mr. Hernandez came along. We walked to Main Beach, which was a bit of a hike, but we had all that food to burn off. My parents walked ahead of us, holding hands.

Grandma and Mr. Hernandez walked behind us. I turned around once to say something to them, but they were kissing passionately. Thankfully, Grandma had her teeth in.

On the way back, I walked with my dad while my mom gave Theo the McBride Inquisition, which meant seemingly innocent questions about school and college plans, but were really questions to find out if he was suitable for her daughter.

I gave her a puzzled look. My family was treating Theo like someone they'd never met before. Then it dawned on me. He'd never been dating their daughter before.

"Mom, you've known Theo forever," I said in a low voice when she'd paused to catch her breath. "Why the sudden interest in his career choice? We've just started *dating*, so knock it off before you scare him."

Later, Theo snuck up behind me and grabbed me. "It'll take more than a mom inquisition to scare me off, you know."

"You heard me?"

He only chuckled. A few minutes later, he was in conversation with my mom again. What can I say? The guy was a glutton for punishment.

Dad wrapped an arm around me.

"I've missed you, Chloe. You and Nina and your mom," he said.

I didn't know how to tell him I had missed him, too. Things had changed and I didn't think they'd ever be the same again.

Then he nodded in Theo's direction. "I like him, Chloe. Always have. I approve."

I was glad Dad was back, but I really didn't want to have a conversation with him about my love life. Okay, almost nonexistent love life, I corrected myself, remembering a few full-body contact incidents with Theo.

I felt this unfamiliar glow, suspiciously like happiness. Part of it was seeing my parents together again. And a tiny part of me hoped that I would start believing in true love once more.

Chapter Twenty-Two

Christmas was finally over. My dad was home and he showed no signs of leaving. I knew he and Mom thought he was back to stay, but I was having a little trouble trusting what was happening right in front of me. But I was thawing to the idea that we might be a real family again.

Even though I knew we weren't friends anymore, I had bought Bridget a gift and it still sat underneath the tree. I didn't know what to do with it, so I waited until I knew she would be gone and left it at her door.

Finally, it was New Year's Eve. New year, new beginning. Maybe even new boyfriend.

Theo was hosting a party and his house wasn't far. If it got to be too much, I could make my escape early. Besides, I was hoping to spend some time with Theo. I'd finally figured out that Theo was everything Alex only pretended to be.

Kayley and I hung out at my house, listening to music and waiting until the party was in full swing before making an appearance. She was sprawled out on the floor.

"Thank you for being honest with me about what you thought of the whole thing with Bridget," I said conversationally.

Kayley sat up.

"But still," I said, "I always got the feeling that you encouraged the whole idea."

Kayley shrugged. "I did."

I sat up, too. "But why?"

"Well, Bridget's kind of a tool sometimes," she said. "And it was always like you let her have anything she wanted. I always thought you could have done better."

"Me?" I asked.

"Yeah, you," she said. "Chloe, I know Bridget was your best friend, but didn't you realize how she put you down?"

Reflexively, I protested. "That's how Bridget is," I said. "She never meant anything by it."

Kayley shook her head. "If you say so," she murmured and dropped the subject. "Time to go."

We got there at about ten o'clock. The party was in full rage mode. Kayley headed for the bar to get us something to drink. She headed for the soft drinks instead of the keg, I noticed.

Theo appeared at my side. "You made it!"

"Hi, Theo," I said. "Kayley convinced me." Theo wore a faded black shirt with the word "Vince" on the front.

"Nice shirt," I said.

"Thanks. I finally got it back from Alex. My favorite movie is —"

I knew what he was going to say, even before he said it. I had fallen for Alex because of a shirt that wasn't even his. He probably hadn't even *seen* the movie.

"*The Color of Money,*" we finished at the same time. I couldn't believe it, but it made sense. Alex had been wearing Theo's shirt at the Halloween party.

He smiled at me.

"It's my favorite movie, too," I said, telling myself that it didn't mean anything. There was more to Theo than a stupid T-shirt, but I was glad that it was his shirt and not Alex's.

"Want to help me pick out some music?" I nodded, and we went over to the stereo system. I flipped through a stack of music and stopped when I came to a Nick Drake CD and remembered my conversation with Theo on the beach.

He noticed me looking at it. Our eyes met and I knew we were both remembering Christmas Eve on the beach. I blushed and dropped my eyes from his.

He took the CD from me and, a minute later, Nick Drake was on the stereo.

Theo said, "Do you want to dance?"

"Sure," I said.

Theo took me into his arms and drew me close. I put my cheek against his shoulder and felt the edge of his collarbone. I breathed in the incredible smell of Theo and thought how easy it would be to stay there, in his arms.

Then the song ended and we broke apart. We stood there, shoulders touching, but not saying anything.

"If you want to get away, we have a pool table in the game room," he said. He hesitated. "Maybe we can play a game later?"

"Sure," I said. I smiled at him. "I'd really like that."

A minute later, there was a crash from one of the upstairs rooms and Theo hurried off.

His mom and her boyfriend were in the family room, sipping margaritas. I went in to say hi, but it was wall-to-wall bodies at the Roussos household and it was hard to talk over the noise.

I said a quick hello and then drifted out. I finally found a quiet little corner to people watch. I wasn't exactly in a party mood, but I didn't want to leave yet. I couldn't take the thought of the alternative, which was spending New Year's Eve with my parents, who were still in their newly reunited, grab-ass-and-giggle phase.

I saw Rich Edmunds, the guy who supposedly had a crush on me, holding hands with a cute redheaded girl. He looked happy.

He caught me staring and gave me a little wave. I waved back, perhaps more enthusiastically than I should have, because he came over to the couch where I sat contemplating my life.

"Hi, Chloe." I braced myself for something, a declaration of love, maybe? "It's nice to see you."

"You, too," I said. There was an awkward silence between us.

"Rich—"

"Yeah, Chloe?" He looked over at the redheaded girl and smiled, then met my eyes. I'd never seen him look so serious. "You know, letting someone in is worth it. Totally worth it."

What had happened to the never-taking-anything-seriously Rich? I couldn't argue with him. He was right. I don't know what he expected me to say, but he was waiting for something.

"How did you get so smart?" I said, nudging him with my shoulder. I was trying to get him to smile, but he looked at me and said, "I'm serious, Chloe."

"You're right, you know," I said. I caught sight of Theo and smiled at him.

"There's hope for you after all, McBride," he said.

"Hi," Kayley said brightly. "You don't mind if I borrow Chloe, do you, Rich?"

I smiled my good-bye as she dragged me off into a corner. "You looked like you needed rescuing," she said. "Are you okay?"

"It was fine," I said. "It seems as though Rich has moved on."

"So I see," Kayley said drily. She jerked her head toward a couch, where Rich sat with his redhead in his lap. Their faces looked like they were glued together.

"It's been difficult for him to get over me," I said with a straight face. "But it would have never worked out between us. I mean, have you *seen* the way he plays pool?"

Kayley burst out laughing.

"Seriously, it was cool to see how he looked at that girl. Like she was everything to him," I said. " I want someone to look at me like that."

"Somebody already does," she said, motioning toward Theo, who was occupied playing host. "But I've been wanting to tell you something about Alex," she said. "Bridget's here with —"

Someone coming in the front door caught Kayley's attention.

"Look who's here," she said. She nudged me.

Alex walked in, followed closely by Bridget. Together again, I saw.

Bridget headed for the keg. But instead of joining her, Alex walked over to a huge wall filled with Roussos family photos.

I went over to say hello.

He studied a photo on the wall like he'd never seen a photograph before.

"Hi, Alex," I said. I smiled. Not even he and Bridget could get to me tonight. "I didn't know you were going to be here."

"Chloe. Hi. I didn't know you would be here either," he said. I waited for him to say something else, but he stared at his feet.

It was obvious he didn't want to be seen talking to me. I wasn't trying to pick him up. I was just trying to be friendly. Bridget gave me a step-away-from-my-man look and I remembered why I hated parties. The ugly side of human nature was revealed at parties. I knew everyone had a bad side, but that didn't mean I wanted to see it out in the open.

Theo had said something about a pool table, so I went in search of it. A couple of games of pool and the night wouldn't be a total loss. I was torn between pretending the cue ball was Alex's face or Bridget's. I could trade off, I decided.

I wandered into the game room. It took me awhile; Theo's house was huge. It was deserted, as long as you ignored the couple writhing on the floor. I did.

The table looked like it hadn't been used in a while, although I was guessing the couple on the floor had been considering putting it to a new and inventive use. On second thought, what they'd been thinking of was probably nothing the table hadn't seen before.

I racked the balls, hoping the couple would get the hint. They did, but only enough to move to a dark corner of the room, where they plopped down on an old leather sofa and resumed groping.

I made the break and watched with satisfaction as several solids went spinning into corner pockets. Solids were my favorite. Superstitious, I know, but there was something so reliable about solids. Stripes were more unpredictable and I'd had enough of unpredictable lately.

At some point, the lechers in the corner staggered away, presumably looking for an unoccupied bedroom.

I was lining up the next shot when Alex came in.

"I thought I'd find you here," he said.

"This is a very nice table," I observed, not looking up.

"Who cares about the table? I wanted to talk to you," he said. "I'm sorry about the way I acted."

"Don't worry about it," I interrupted him. I took careful aim with my cue and was surprised to see that my hands were completely steady.

"Bridget and I got together way before . . ."

I whacked the ball hard. It skittered away, missing the seven by about a mile.

I drew a breath. "Way before what?" I asked.

"Way before us," Alex said.

"There is no us," I said. It was true. There wasn't. Not anymore.

He stood there a few minutes, but when I wouldn't talk to him or even look at him, he finally left.

I spent about a minute pretending the eight ball was stupid Alex's face.

"I saw Alex come in here," Theo said. "Was he bothering you?"

The sight of him made me feel better. "No, apologizing, if you can believe it."

"Are you okay?"

"I'm fine." I took another shot and then looked up. Theo was frowning. "He's ancient history. What time is it, anyway?"

"Almost midnight."

I smiled. "Then what are you doing so far away?"

We started early on the countdown kiss. Best midnight kiss ever.

Chapter Twenty-Three

I was trying to keep my New Year's resolution, which was to win the tournament.

I wandered downstairs. My parents were at the breakfast table, nuzzling and giggling like newlyweds.

"Please, not before breakfast," I said. But I was kidding. I was glad they were happy. I just didn't need to see it before I had my Wheaties. I grabbed a bowl of cereal and sat with them.

"Did you have fun last night, honey?" Dad asked. It seemed a little surreal to have him back at home, but both my parents were glowing.

I had decided I'd forget that Alex had been wearing Bridget like a cheap sombrero last night. I thought I'd been doing my Great Pretender act pretty well. My mother's next comment proved how wrong I was.

"What's the matter? Didn't you have fun at Theo's party?" Mom said.

"Oh, I had fun, all right," I said. "Until Bridget showed up with Alex."

My mom frowned at my tone. She thought Bridget was an angel. "I don't know why you two girls haven't been getting along. You practically shared the same crib."

"Don't remind me. I didn't like sharing then and I don't like it now. Especially not with Bridget." I put my spoon down. My cereal was soggy and unappealing. "Bridget and I are over."

My mom made a little distressed noise. "It's okay, Mom. I'm going to meet Kayley," I said. Well, I would be, as soon as I called her. I wanted to find out what happened at the party after I left. I don't know why I couldn't leave it alone, but I couldn't. The thought of Alex and Bridget still made me want to spew my Wheaties, but only because I'd been hustled.

I drove downtown and found a place to park right away. Finding a parking spot improved my mood, because parking in Laguna was a bitch.

We met at the Corner Café. Surprisingly, she was there before me, sitting in a corner booth. She looked beautiful in a sweater that matched her blue eyes.

I waved to her and then went to stand in line. There was a teapot in front of Kayley so I knew she'd already ordered. I ordered an extra large vanilla latte because I had a feeling I'd need the caffeine.

"So how was the rest of the party?" I said, casually.

"You and Theo disappeared," she commented.

"Countdown kiss." I blushed. "I didn't feel like an audience."

"What?" she shrieked in my ear. "You guys seem to be getting serious. When were you going to tell me?"

She looked at my face. I tried not to show any emotion, but Kayley was psychic or something when it came to my love life.

"I knew it," she said. "You and Theo. He wasn't interested in anybody but you," she said.

I positively beamed at her. "Thanks a lot." I don't know why, but I felt like hugging her.

I started to say something else, but Vinnie came up and slid his arms around her waist. "Hi, there," he said, kissing her. I raised an eyebrow.

"Hang on a minute," she said to him, but then leaned closer to me and whispered, "You two are perfect together. Theo's a nice guy. And, well, Alex isn't. He's a creep who uses people."

She got up to leave. "Call me later if you want to talk," she added.

I sat there and sipped my drink, thinking about everything Kayley had told me. I was getting up to leave when I looked through the window and saw Bridget and Alex stroll by, hand in hand.

I was surprised I didn't feel more than a little sadness. After a few minutes, I walked over to Gino's. Seeing Alex and Bridget together reminded me I needed to practice. Theo had been a huge distraction and the tournament was only days away.

The tables at Gino's were all in use. I glared at a particularly PDA-prone couple who were spending more time exchanging saliva than playing any real pool.

They finally left and I snagged their table. I shot a game or two, but my mind was on Theo.

I popped a ball off the table and sent it flying. It almost brained this freshman with braces, but he ducked at the last minute.

I went over to pick up the ball. "Sorry," I said to him. He mumbled something about chicks not knowing how to play pool. Normally, I'd jump down his throat for a comment like that, but it was my fault, after all.

That's what I got for letting a guy distract me. I was hoping fate would make it easy for me and Theo would walk into Gino's. I kept looking over my shoulder, waiting for him to appear. I put my cue away and grabbed one of the cues Gino had for the tourists to use.

Although I hung around until almost dinnertime, Theo didn't magically appear.

Chapter Twenty-Four

Mom was waiting for me when I got home. What now? I was surprised when she handed me a check.

"What's this for?"

"I want to sponsor you in the tournament."

"But what about Dad? He sponsored Alex."

She sighed. "Your father doesn't get it sometimes. He didn't mean to hurt our feelings. He just . . ."

"Didn't think. He loves the attention, just like Alex."

"No, not like Alex," she said. "Your dad may love the attention, but he loves us more. And I'm thrilled he's working again."

I looked down, embarrassed that my mom knew I made fun of Dad's designer pieces.

"I can tell he's thrilled to be home," I said. Somehow, talking to my mom made me realize that I couldn't control anybody else's life, just my own. And it was time I started worrying about my own life instead of my parents'. I thought they'd be fine, but even if they weren't, it wasn't my problem.

I should have been working on my game. How else was I going to beat Alex's ass? I hoped I could, but I couldn't be sure. There was only one way to tell.

My grandmother came over for lunch the next day. She actually took over lunch.

I wished Nina were home to help me deal. I loved Grandma, but she could be a handful, and Mr. Hernandez wasn't there to bring out her softer side.

She could cook, however. We sat down to tender salmon, wild rice, and asparagus.

"Where's that young man we met at Christmas?" Grandma said.

"Mom, I don't think —"

"Suzy, I wasn't talking to you." My mom's name is Susan, but Grandma insisted on using her childhood nickname, even though she knew Mom hated it.

"He's not my boyfriend," I said baldly. "He's just a friend."

"Bound to happen. Gorgeous boy like that needs to sow his oats."

"Grandma, Theo's not like that."

Grandma harrumphed a bit, but I relaxed when she, fortunately, lost interest in my love life.

"When are you going to let me teach you to cook?" Thankfully, my mouth was full of rice when Grandma asked me the question.

"She's busy right now," my mom said. "She's practicing for a pool tournament."

"Pool? In my day, decent girls didn't play pool," Grandma said. "What do you want to play pool for, anyway? You'll never get a boy playing pool."

"Grandma, I'm good at pool," I said, swallowing the lump in my throat. "And who says I want a boyfriend right now?"

She cackled. "That's what girls who can't get one always say. No boy wants a girl who can beat him. At pool or anything else."

My dad started to say something, but my mom put a hand on his arm.

She said, "Mom, that's enough. I won't have you discouraging Chloe the way you discouraged me."

"The girl needs to hear it. How is she going to get a man?"

My dad glanced at me. I was biting my tongue. I didn't want to say anything to Grandma. She was almost eighty.

"Can I be excused?"

My mom nodded and I left the room. I could hear Grandma's voice, getting louder and louder as I went up the stairs. So much for a quiet family meal.

What did Grandma think I should do, anyway? Lose the tournament? Theo didn't care if I competed in the tournament. The whole idea that a guy would be freaked out about a girl playing pool was archaic.

Although Grandma's comments were annoying, I felt like everything was finally coming together for me. I'd lost Bridget, but I'd found Kayley.

Theo and I seemed to be meshing as well. I decided to call him. About twenty minutes after my phone call, we were alone in Theo's house and it seemed natural to be kissing him on his living room couch. It was the only place I wanted to be at that moment, but he didn't seem to think so.

"I don't know what you saw in him," he said against my mouth.

"Who?" I kissed his neck.

Theo sat up. "Alex."

I stifled a groan. "Do we have to talk about this right this second?" I ran my fingers under his shirt, along his spine. I was intent on taking advantage of his mom's absence. Alex was the last thing on my mind. What I had felt for Alex, whatever that was, seemed as far away as if it had happened to someone else.

"Yes, we do." Theo gently but firmly removed my hands from his body. "Now, tell me why this tournament is so important to you."

Why was he making a big deal of this?

"Theo," I said, jumping off the couch, "sometimes a tournament is just a tournament."

His reply stopped me at the door. "And sometimes it's not. Tell me what's really going on with you. You've been obsessed with winning."

My answer was to slam his front door hard and head for home.

Chapter Twenty-Five

The first round of the tournament was that Saturday, but my game wasn't until late in the day. Nina, as usual, was studying, but promised to show up for Sunday's final matches.

"Knock 'em dead," Dad said.

There was a crowd gathered when I walked into Gino's, but thankfully, no sign of either Alex or Bridget.

I was playing some guy from Laguna Hills High School. His name was Brent and he was supposed to be good, but I thought I could take him.

He took the break and got solids. I got stripes, which I thought were unlucky for me. I was convinced of it, which is why he almost ran the table before I figured out I should stop being superstitious and just play. I made the next shot and ended his lucky streak.

I won the match, but not by much. I could have let him win, and that way, I wouldn't have to play Alex. I wouldn't have to look across the table and see his gorgeous, deceptive face. But there was no way I was going to do that.

Kayley would have never let me forget it, and besides, I was determined to beat Alex at his own game. After all, it was about time I stood up for myself.

The two thousand dollar prize would now go directly toward my car expense fund, since my parents were making me pay for the insurance. Not that I minded. I loved my little car.

Brent seemed fine with the loss and even shook my hand afterward. "Good game, McBride. But watch out. I'll be coming after you next year."

I grinned at him. "I'll be ready."

Kayley came up after Brent walked away.

"You know what you have to do now, right?" she said.

"Beat the pants off Alex," I said, "and finally end this thing with Bridget."

"Rack 'em and crack 'em," she said. And I wasn't sure that she was talking about pool.

Now if I could get my former best friend, Bridget, to stop using me as her personal scratching post. I knew I deserved some of those claws, but it didn't make the digs any less painful.

Kayley was right. When I left Gino's, I knew what I had to do. I went home and got some sleep. I had a pool tournament to win.

The final game for the tournament was scheduled

for Sunday afternoon. I didn't see Bridget before the event. But my parents insisted on showing up for the final tournament game. I carefully packed my new stick and made sure I had everything I needed.

The place was packed. It looked like every kid in my high school had shown up. I saw Kayley sitting at a booth with Theo and Vinnie.

"What's going on?" I said. "Why are there so many kids from school here?"

"Bridget opened her big mouth. She told everyone and now it's all over the school. Everyone is here to see if Alex will beat you. Rumor is that if you win, Alex is the prize."

"Just what I need. An audience of Bridget's adoring fans."

Kayley nodded, then stood and gave me a quick hug. "Rack 'em and crack 'em," she said again.

I grinned at her and some of the butterflies in my stomach settled down.

Bridget was already there, sitting with Lia Cruz. Bridget wore a shimmering silver top and a pair of shiny heels that looked like she could impale someone with them. Probably me, I thought gloomily.

A few minutes later, Alex walked in. He was wearing a black shirt that exactly matched his hair. I pictured him trying on several choices, looking in the mirror before deciding on the one that made his black hair gleam even more.

"How about a kiss for luck?" he said. The sad thing was that I still wasn't sure who he was talking to. Maybe he wasn't sure either, but Bridget stood and gave him a peck on the cheek.

He smiled and then went over to talk to his uncle, which left Bridget and me alone.

"He was talking to *me*," Bridget said. "He won't want you anyway, not if you beat him. He's going to win either way, but take my advice and withdraw now while you still can."

"Go screw yourself," I said, smiling widely with gritted teeth.

She said, "Either way, you lose. I'm going to get what I want. I always do."

She walked away and stood in the opposite corner. I muttered, "Not this time, you won't."

Theo came over and took my arm. "Chloe, I need to talk to you for a minute." He guided me over to a semi-quiet corner.

I looked at him, but he didn't say anything for a minute.

Finally, he said, "Look, I know you think that you have to win, but would it be so bad if you didn't get Prince Charming over there?"

"That's not the point," I said. "If Alex can't take being beat by a girl, I *really* don't want him anyway."

"I thought so," he said, before he stomped off.

He hadn't given me time to tell him that I didn't

want Alex at all. I wanted that two thousand dollar prize. I wanted to prove to myself that I could win.

I was going to play my best and hope I had enough faith in myself for it to work. My stomach rumbled, my palms sweated, and I felt like I might throw up the cereal I'd had for breakfast.

When I started all this, I didn't realize that there was more at stake than just a guy. I didn't know that I was betting on the strength of a fourteen-year friendship.

Gino lumbered out of the kitchen and sat down with Bridget to watch. Gino's familiar presence comforted me, but I marveled that two people from the same family could be so different. I'd been through so much with Alex; I'd practically forgotten he was related to Gino.

I looked across the pool table at Alex. He looked calm and leaned casually against the arm of a chair.

We flipped for the break, but Alex took it. The balls scattered and two of his went in.

He smiled triumphantly at me, took aim, and made a bank shot. It wasn't the easiest shot in the world. The bank shot that I taught him, I remembered bitterly.

He wiped his brow. He's nervous, I thought, which gave me some satisfaction. He should be. But then he made the next shot and then the next.

Bridget ran over to Alex and gave him a lingering

kiss. When they emerged from the clinch, she looked over to make sure I had been watching.

She was trying to shark me, but I wouldn't let myself be distracted. It didn't bother me that she was kissing him. I didn't like him anymore. He wasn't who I had thought he was, but it hurt that Bridget wanted me to lose the game.

Then it occurred to me. Maybe Bridget had a different reason for wanting to win than I did. Maybe she didn't care about the game. Maybe she cared about Alex, cared about him more than I did.

My stomach churned. I'd never thought that Alex would actually have a chance at winning the tournament, but he was good. He actually had a chance.

NO way was he going to win. He wasn't going to be given the chance. I'd wipe the table with him before he even thought about winning.

But I miscalculated the angle of my next shot, gave it too much English, and missed. There was a nervous twitch in my stomach. In all probability, my mistake had cost me the tournament. Nina gave me the thumbs-up and an encouraging smile, but I was too nervous to smile back at her.

Then it was Alex's turn and he missed his shot. I was still in the game.

There were three balls on the table. One stripe, mine. One solid, Alex's. And the eight ball. I took a deep breath. Past conversations swirled around in my head.

He still had that cocky grin on his face. My first impulse was to wipe it off. I knew my best chance to win was to knock the thirteen ball into the center left, but I hesitated.

I squared my chin and stalked to the table. I remembered to stay down on the shot and sunk the last of the stripes into the center left pocket, clean and cool. One shot left. The eight ball was lined up perfectly. Practically impossible to miss, but my hands were shaking.

I glanced over at Bridget. Her head was down and she was biting her nails. I couldn't see her face behind her hair. She wanted him to win, not to beat me, but because she loved him. It was time to end the game.

I walked closer to Bridget, pretending to study the table for my shot. But what I really wanted was to get within hearing distance.

"He's the consolation prize," I said.

"What did you say?" she responded, swinging around.

I bent down, looking at the angle of the shot. "I said that he's your consolation prize. I mean, when I win the tournament. I don't want him enough to let him ruin our friendship."

For a minute, the old Bridget was there. She beamed at me, started to throw her arms around me, but stopped herself at the last minute.

"I love him, you know," she said in a low voice.

"I know," I said. "And I hope he loves you, too."

I surveyed the table and tapped the left corner pocket, calling my shot.

The shot cracked, the sound ringing in my ears. I held my breath as it slowly, oh-so-slowly made its way to the corner pocket. The ball seemed to hesitate, rotating a little, until it sunk like a stone into the corner pocket.

I had won the tournament.

I looked around for Theo, but couldn't see him through the crowd of clapping people who had surrounded the table. Then I saw him. His face was white, and he looked like someone had elbowed him in the stomach or something. I took a step forward, but he turned and walked out the door.

Mom and Dad were there to cheer me on. Dad practically bolted across the room and then wrapped his arms around me and twirled me around.

"You did it, honey! We're so proud." I smiled up at Dad, gave him a hug, and laughed when he spun me again.

Gino came over and shook my hand. "Congratulations, Chloe. Great game. You're a very intuitive player, probably the most intuitive I've seen. I thought you were in trouble for a minute there, but you stayed with it."

He presented me with a check. "Put that in your college fund. I hear there are some great college tournaments," he said, before heading back to the kitchen.

I stared at the check for two thousand dollars.

The crowd thinned out. Across the pool table, I saw Alex. Our glances met and held for a minute, but then he looked away. And then Bridget went over to him and whispered in his ear. They looked right together. It gave me a pang, but I knew I'd done the right thing.

I had hoped that it was still possible to regain a part of my friendship with Bridget, but she left without a backward glance, hand in hand with Alex.

"Hey, Chloe," someone yelled. "Your boyfriend is walking out with someone else."

I ignored them. I didn't care what the people at school thought. Except for Theo. I stared at the piece of paper in my hand. I'd won the tournament, but I'd lost even more. Theo was gone and he wasn't coming back. At least not to me. I raced after him.

"I didn't tell you, but Bridget and I had already decided that Alex was going to be the consolation prize. So I had to win that game or I would have been stuck with him."

Theo stopped in his tracks. "You made me go through the agony of watching that game, wondering if you were going to sink the eight ball and waltz out of there with that jerk?" Theo grinned. "Well, I'm glad he was the consolation prize. I have plans for you."

He kissed me and then said, "Big plans."

Kayley and Vinnie were still sitting in a booth at the back of Gino's. She had her head on his shoulder.

"We're going over to Theo's house," I said.

Kayley's head snapped up.

I looked her in the eyes. "We're going to shoot some pool. That's it."

She put her head back down on Vinnie's shoulder. "Have fun," she said, "but not too much fun."

The last part was for Theo's benefit, I'm sure.

Kayley winked at me as we left. "Be good," she whispered, "but not too good."

My stomach fluttered as I thought about being alone with Theo.

When we got to his house, we tiptoed to the game room. The lights were low. I stood by the pool table, feeling awkward.

Theo reached for me and I knew all bets were off.

"I thought we were going to play pool," I said.

"We are," he promised, "but there's more to life than pool."

He cupped my face in his hands and my pulse sped up, anticipating a kiss. But he cradled my face, his thumb tracing the line of my jaw before finally bending down to kiss me, a long, slow kiss. He tasted like chocolate and possibilities.

I realized he was right, that there was more to life than pool. "This *is* much better than pool," I murmured.

Theo choked back a laugh. "I didn't think you thought there was anything better than pool."

"That was before I found you," I said.

"Which would you rather do? The pool table is right there. We could play a few games."

I looked from Theo's laughing face to the gleaming table in the center of the room. I smiled and took my shot. Love in the corner pocket, I thought, right where it belongs.

To Do List: Read all the Point books!

By Aimee Friedman

- ☐ South Beach
- ☐ French Kiss
- ☐ Hollywood Hills
- ☐ The Year My Sister Got Lucky

- ☐ Airhead
  By Meg Cabot

- ☐ Suite Scarlett
  By Maureen Johnson

- ☐ Love in the Corner Pocket
  By Marlene Perez

- ☐ Hotlanta
  By Denene Millner
  and Mitzi Miller

Summer Boys series by Hailey Abbott

- ☐ Summer Boys
- ☐ Next Summer
- ☐ After Summer
- ☐ Last Summer

In or Out series by Claudia Gabel

- ☐ In or Out
- ☐ Loves Me, Loves Me Not
- ☐ Sweet and Vicious
- ☐ Friends Close, Enemies Closer

- ☐ Orange Is the New Pink
  By Nina Malkin

Making a Splash series by Jade Parker

- ☐ Robyn
- ☐ Caitlin
- ☐ Whitney

Once Upon a Prom series by Jeanine Le Ny

- ☐ Dream
- ☐ Dress
- ☐ Date

PNTLST3

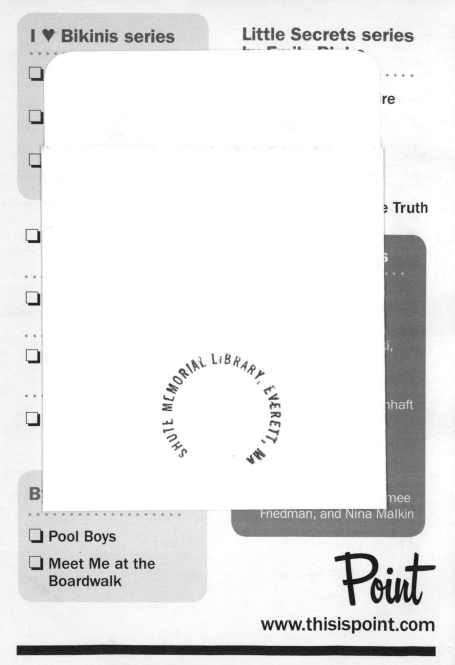

I ♥ Bikinis series

❏

❏

❏

❏

❏

❏

❏

Little Secrets series

re

Truth

ki,

nhaft

B

mee
Friedman, and Nina Malkin

❏ Pool Boys

❏ Meet Me at the
Boardwalk

Point

www.thisispoint.com